Itchycooblue

DES DILLON

itchycooblue

DES DILLON

review

First published in 1999
by REVIEW

An imprint of Headline Book Publishing

10 9 8 7 6 5 4 3 2 1

ISBN 0 7427 7546 7

Printed and bound in Great Britain by
Clays Ltd, St Ives plc

Headline Book Publishing
A division of Hodder Headline PLC
338 Euston Road
London NW1 3BH

For Joseph Nicola Daniel Darrell Allan
all mad in their own wee ways

And Joanne – mad for putting up wi me.

Ziiiiing!

See me. See ma magination. WILD. I won't take a tellin me
so I won't. Nope. I just let ma head run away wi me. Get me
into bother one day ma teacher says. Right bother so it will.

Derrick Daniel Riley, would you PLEASE *stop daydreaming
and answer the question,* Trimmer goes this day when I'm
lookin at big dinosaurs in telephone boxes in the clouds. Her
voice sounds like it's talkin to somebody in ma chair that's
not me. Ma brain's outside the windae lookin at the Peak
stickin up above the houses. It's like the mountain on the
Dracula film. Transilvaynia. An behind it in the distance the
cars're whizzin by on the jewel carriageway. Whizzzz.
Whizzzz. Whizzzz.

SALAP P P P P P
SALAP P P P P P

Tweety Pies're doin a merry-go-round in ma head. An
stars're spinnin outside ma skull like satellites.

Come in Kennedy Derrick's just been skelped. Twice! It looks
like the Shows on a rainy night. All blurry red an yella. All

loud noises an singin in yer ears an spinnin lights. An music.
Ma head's shakin to a stop an the rain on the glass's runnin
in trickles like wee planets that's fell out the Solar System.
Ma eyes're startin to see her voice poundin off the walls an
everybody else's behind curved arms an sticky up pencils.
Ye'd think I'd be makin up excuses. But I'm not. *It always
rains when the Shows come,* the raindrops're sayin in secret
rain language.

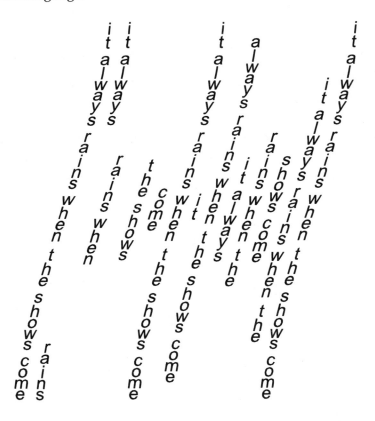

It always rains when the Shows come. It's a whisper.
   There the Shows, ma maw always says an looks at the sky
an tells all us to run out an bring in that washin an she'd be

shovin a outsider on Jam in her face an sccclurpin tea. *It'll be rainin afore the day's out,* she'd go burblin into her mug. *Mark ma words.* How'd'ye mark words? Wi an invisible air pen?

There ma head's away again. I'm just supposed to tell ye about the last story I tolt ye. Called Me an Ma Gal. Ma new second-year teacher says it's a packet of lies. Fikshun. Me an Gal never nearly got muddered an abyoosed in the trees by Strangler Joe. He's a figmint of ma magination. An ma magination'll get me in trouble some day. So that's it. Packet of lies. Porkie Pies. None of it ever happened. There!

Pssst!

PSST! LISTEN! See all that stuff on the last page I wrote? All about Strangler Joe not bein real? Well that's all lies. Strangler Joe *was* real. Trimmer made me do it. She read ma story out an got them to laugh at me. I sayed it's all real an she battered me. Whackin me on the napper wi first-year jotters. Joanne Brennan was behind me. I'm beetroot an Trimmer holds ma jotter up by the corner like it's a shitty nappy.

THIS, CHILDREN...

She shakes it about a bit.

This is what happens, children, when we give free rein to our Imagination!

That made me think ma magination was four horses an I'm tryin to pull them back. But the reins're diggin in ma hands so I let them go an clippity clop off they pop over rivers an through forests an up the blue sky wi big white wings sproutin out their sides.

OUT!!! She goes an makes me stand at the blackboard. All the lassies're lookin through their fringes.

She clip clops over the shiny floor an drops the shitty nappy in the bin. They all look at that then me like I forgot ma trousers an Ys. I even look down to check. Yup. No bare arse. Ever had that dream? You're in the free dinner queue an all these fourth years're pointin an howlin like banshees at yer willie curlin up? I get it all the time. I hate bein a free dinner. Ma da can't get a job the now. He can't work anymore cos of the roofs. Before he worked on the concrete he worked on the roofs. Sheetin. But he breathes funny now. He's got Bestos. Sometimes he's good sometimes he's bad. But things're pickin up he says. Won't be long now. Get a job anywhere ma da. There's nothin about roofs he doesn't know. We might be goin to Anstruther. Good for his lungs.

Yer da canny get a job without a dummy tit, they sometimes sing at me.

Don't bother wi them, ma maw says, *Half of them don't even know who their da is. There'd be trouble in this town if everybody knew their da. Aye – big trouble!* She always goes when she's walkin away – *Ye can always tell yer mother but ye can't tell yer da.*

But where am I? That's right. Strangler Joe. He was real. But I've to kid on he's not. That's what Trimmer wants. But I'm tellin you it all happened. If ye're ever in Columba there's a wee English Teacher wi hair like a boy – that's Trimmer. Don't tell her I sayed Strangler Joe was real.

It's been ages since Strangler Joe. Gal's at Columba now an all. First-year. We're still pals but. Things're always happenin to me an Gal. I could tell ye a million stories. But I've got to tell ye about what happened the time ma da went into a tent. Mackenzie was after us.

Daylight Robbery at Night

So! This night I'm at ma windae. I've been there ages cos ma maw an da's in SOME MOOD. The Telly Meter man came an there was nothin in it. He's takin it away if it happens again. No more DON'T WATCH ALONE that means. WHOAAAAAHHH!!! The Wolfman!

I'm playin wi plasticine. I like playin wi plasticine. Even if I am second year. Magination. That's how I like it. Most boys like football an Joe Ninety stuff – or even Spacehoppers – but give me a lump of plasticine an I'm happy all day.

Give Derrick a lump of plasticine and he's happy all day! ma primary teacher sayed to ma maw once. Parents' night. I turns an smiles at ma maw. Glowin I was. Spectin ma maw to be grinnin or mibbi a wee magic twinkle of her nose. Like Bewitched. Samantha. But she breathes in deep an she's got her left eye on me an her other eye's twistin round her nose. The teacher goes *ahem ahem,* an flicks bits of paper. Ma belly starts fallin off a cliff. Can't figure out why. Sometimes ma belly knows there's somethin bad before me.

But she's quick Miss Boswell. Nifty. She smiles wi an idea. The only thing missin's the bulb above her head. BING! She lifts up this **thing** made out paper mashy an crepe paper an buttons an Hands That Do Dishes bottles an shoves it over to ma Maw. It's like a pigsty that's blew up.

They start goin on about how good it is. I don't even know what it is. I stuck all these things thegether an took them into school. Miss Boswell comes up an says, *Is that a space station Derrick?* An I goes, *Aye, I mean Yes Miss Boswell.* An she tells me it's a great space station pokin at all the bits an noddin like the dog in the back of ma uncle Eddie's car.

So it's a space station. Ma maw sniffs hunners of air in her nose an forgets all the stuff about plasticine an daftness.

It was Blue Peter but the meter ran out. Valerie Simpleton – that's what Gal calls her – I got the paper mashy thegether an **bing!** – it's a wee white dot.

I made the rest up when ma maw was lookin for the scissors to put it back on. But I had the scissors. So when she's goin mental an I realises I've got them – I stuffs them down the couch.

She goes spare. She gets ma da to shout us up to bed. *Caroline Derrick Linda Angie Stevie Geddy Wendy Donna David $B - E - D$.* He could hardly breathe after that. Bed early. Nobody's ownin up to the scissors. Specially me. Ma da used to tuck us into bed before he started sleepin in the livin room. He used to sing us to sleep. *Rockin Rollin Ridin,* he'd sing, *right along the bay.*

𝄞 *Driver at the engine*
fireman rings the bell
sandman swings his lantern
to show that all is well
rockin rollin ridin
out along the bay
all bound for mornin town
many miles away.

An I loved it cos it was all about trains an me an Gal couldn't get enough of trains. By the way – in case ye're wonderin what the scissors're for – ma da used them to open the telly meter. TeleBank it was called. The guy came to empty it every month. But ma maw an da opened it all the time an took the two bob bits out for messages or five Senior Service. But these days it's mostly cough bottles for ma da. An Victory Vees. Ye just stick the point of the scissors in the lock an wiggle them about givin it a wee turn at the same time an bingo the lock swings opened. TeleBank comes to empty it an ma maw stuffs a tenner in the night before. Nice as ye like he opens it an pulls out the tenner, fills in his wee forms an he's offski. Never a word about how did ye manage to get a ten pound note in the wee two bob slot?

Next thing ma maw tears in the room an sets about me wi a rubber glove. She's got a pint tumbler full of Hands That Do Dishes in her other hand. It's sloppin all over the place. She's nearly greetin like it's the end of the world. She drags me down to ma da by the hair. All I can see is the blank screen on the Telly.

That's the fifth time Pat! she's goin but ma da's findin it hard to breathe.

You're not watchin that Blue Peter again, she goes. Ma da's noddin his head like he's fed up.

I found five Fairy Liquid bottles under his bed! She stands wi
the folded arms that mean *Are you not goin to get out yer bed
an slap this boy about?*

He leans forwards an slaps me a couple of times on the
head. It's not sore. He's good at that ma Da. Slappin ye loud
but ye don't feel nothin. Septic's da can't. His face's puffed
up black an blue for days sometimes. Gal says he can't see
the slaps comin cos his eyes're on the run from each other.

*Ma heart's roasted wi him Pat. Roasted. He'll have me in
Heartwood so he will.* Ma maw's always sayin that. I used to
think yer heart got roasted an turned into a big lump of black
burnt wood. Then ye went to Heartwood an they got it soft
an put the fire out. But Gal's brothers' laughed their heads
off when I told them. Bendin over like stumic pain. They
sayed it's a Loony Bin. What's ma maw on about then? She's
not a loony. I don't know what's goin on sometimes.

But there it's away already. Ma head. Mibbi I'm a loony!
Mibbi it's me that's goin to Heartwood. I'm tryin to tell ye
about the time Mackenzie was after me an Gal.

What was I on about? Aw right – the plasticine. I'm at the
windae this night an it's plasticine I've got. Ye can make
anythin. Planes. UFOs. Dolifins. Celtic. Rangers. Anythin.
But this night it's Gigantor. He's on the Telly. A cartoon. He
comes flyin out the sky shoutin,

GIIIIIIIIII GAAAAAAAAAAN TORRRRRRR

every time somebody's trapped. Same as Superman. I get
him to save all the other plasticine people. I make hearts an
stumics an wee brains in their heads. Then I give them
needles for sords. I make them fence each other to bits. When
they're all stabbed up I rush them to hospital an slice them
open wi a Wilkinson Sord. They're the best blades in the
world. If they've got holes in their brains or hearts when I
open them I count them as dead. Sometimes the sord only
punctures the skin – couple of stitches an they're swishin the
Wilkinson's about in no time. They look up at the sky an

GIIIIIIIIII GAAAAAAAAAAN TORRRRRRR

comes swoopin down an bumps them on the floor. Dead. Squashed like accordions. He never meant it Gigantor. But sometimes the goodies died an ye couldn't save them. That's the way it was. That's the way the cookie crumbles so it is. *There's people dyin now that's never died before,* is what ma Granda Riley used to say.

Oh Danny that's Lizzie Duffy died there.

Well – there's people dyin now that's never died before, he'd go.

Know how they tell ye the news at the beginnin an then tell ye it all again, only longer, after the music? News At Ten.

BONGGGGGGGGGGGGGGGG

The guy says – *Big Robot kills six.*

Can ye magine ma da's face at that bit? His eyebrows tryin to swap places wi each other.

BONGGGGGGGGGGGGGGGG

There's that Gigantor kilt six people Pat! ma maw'd go.

BONGGGGGGGGGGGGGGGG

Aye – I always knew there was more to him than met the eye, she says, *supposed to be a goodie. His eyes are a bit close thegether for a metal guy that Gigantor fellah. Hmph. Some goodie. A bad article. A right bad article. An his father was just the same.*

BONGGGGGGGGGGGGGGGG

But that's all made up in ma head. This is what really happened. Ma maw crashed in the room an goes, *He's a right rotten bastard that Gigantor he's kilt six goodies.*

Only kiddin. That never happened either. I'm at the windae an my eyes're on Gigantor. Then on rain slidin down the glass. This one's like a wee bubble car steerin in an out the stopped ones. Somethin funny's in it. Inside the bubble car raindrop. It's Sonny Hammil's van. Sonny Hammil's van's in the bubble tryin to get out. It's movin up an down the inside walls of the raindrop pushin jaggy corners out. Stretchin. I can hear the squeaks as it tries to press out. I push against the glass an ma nostrils're blowin two triangles of bulls breath down to the sill.

Across the road Sonny Hammil's van's rockin about. Then it's

DEAD STILL

Then it moves from

SIDE

TO

SIDE

That's when I noticed Septic. An this ASDA trolley. ASDA is just opened Up The Street. Ye can get Galbraiths in it six times. Gal says wanes get lost in it. Five've went missin. His Jim puts Rod Stewart tapes down his socks an walks out. *Good job it's not LPs,* Gal says. That's a pisser. Can ye magine it? Jim Gal wi a big square in his flares tryin to sneak out.

Hey where're ye goin wi them big squares in yer flares!!?? big Malloy'd shout. He's the bouncer in ASDA. Ye need a bouncer. People go in just to wander about it's that big. Jim Gal's maw'd wipe the floor wi him if she knew he was shopliftin.

Watch the pies our Jim found two fingers in a pie out ASDA, says Gal. Ye can get everythin there – clothes an plastic sandals an anoraks. Doc's. Parkas. LP's. Stuff that's froze. Cakes an chickens. But we've not got a fridge.

What do I want a fridge for wi youse like a bunch of wolfs? ma maw always says. They shut down all the other shops Up The Street cos ye only need to go to ASDA now. Sonny Hammil had a shop.

Trolleys're good. We love them. We hurl each other down the road an fling them in the Burn that goes under the road above it. Septic wheels dogs on the jewel carriageway an runs. I seen this dog once an it liked it. Cars were swervin everywhere an it was grinnin. It was Muttley out Wacky Races. Swear!

Rassin fassin. Rassin fassin, woofity woof, it was sayin. King of the road.

But this night Septic's eyes're all over the place cos Sonny Hammil'd kill him. He's mad Sonny Hammil. Next minute THUMP. The skylight flaps on the roof. Dead loud. Septic's terryfied. I can see the white bits of his eyes dartin about in the yella lampies.

This hand appears out the roof. It's Mackenzie. I can tell just by the army jacket. Septic's his best pal like me an Gal. If ye see an army jacket doin somethin crazy it's Mackenzie. He's men tal. But he's in the Mary's. Everybody knows that.

Thunk – this box of Mint Cracknells lands on the roof. Thunk MB bars. Thunk Asteks. Thunk Flyin saucers. No Gigantor in sight. Just Septic edgin the trolley closer to the van. *He's got a face ye want to punch,* that's what Gal says his Jim says. His Jim done Septic in for nothin this night for bein born just.

One eye goin to the shops for the messages an the other one comin back wi the change's what Jim always says about Septic. I usually felt sorry for him.

I felt sorry for him cos he was mingin. His maw stands outside the Woodside wi black spaces in her teeth. Drinkin wi these men that always laugh. If I met ma maw down the shops she'd go *Hi Yi son – how's yer da?* But not aul Marian. Whack!!!! an she'd boot Septic up the arse an watch him howl all the way up Wine Alley. It was a different feelin sorry from the feelin sorry for they Thalidomides wi arms comin out everywhere an hands where their soldiers should be. I sometimes called them Thlids an laughed. But I blessed maself when nobody was lookin. In where ma belly is felt like lead. Same wi Spazzys. I only do it when there's people there. If it was just me an a Thalidomide or a Spazzy I'd run down the shops an everythin for them. I'd not laugh or nothin. I'd push their wheelchairs anywhere. That's me. But I don't tell nobody about that. Just you. Ye'd get a doin for wantin to be nice to Spazzies an Thlids in our bit.

But you don't want to know about all that. You want to know about Sonny Hammil's van.

All these boxes're on the roof an Mackenzie squeezes out the skylight. He's like playdough squeezin out the square hole machine. His face's strainin back an his jacket's stretchin. He springs on the roof an stands wi his legs apart like All Because The Lady Loves Milk Tray. He starts chuckin stuff an Septic's catchin it an puttin it in the trolley. Sonny Hammil's probably sittin watchin the news not knowin nothin.

BONGGGGGGGGGGGGGGGG

Now here's the news. In Coatbridge right now Sonny Hammil's van's bein robbed stupit by Septic an Mackenzie who's escaped out the Mary's.

BONGGGGGGGGGGGGGGGG

Can ye magine it? Sonny Hammil's baldy head swingin like Candid Camera. Then screamin out the back door chuckin mops pails an metal milk crates.

Septic's laughin wi nerves an loadin stuff. I've got the light on so if Mackenzie looks up he'll get blinded. A hunner watt! *Good as havin a heater in yer room,* ma da says. It's only me an David an Stevie in that room. In winter there's these white ferns on the glass. Mad. How they get up there I don't know. They always melted in the mornin. I used to think this

Jack Frost World Of White had trees an plants an birds an ferns all made out ice. When he walks by yer house his Jack Frost World Of White tornadoes behind an the shape of it sticks to the glass. But ma maw says I'm as Irish as the pigs of Docherty an, *Don't be daft an mind an empty the bins an wear that big army coat to bed the night.*

Chuck another horse blanket on the bed. That's what ma da calls the army blankets. Ye could sandpaper yer face wi them.

Mackenzie's face's a pile of jaggy rocks an his hair's an aul boggin mop flopped on the top. *Even his pram was camel fladge,* Gal says. He's seen a picture. Mackenzie in his army baby clothes an wee polished boots swearin at his maw. *Leeft right leeft right,* he was shoutin at Big Wilma pushin the pram Jim Gal says.

Anyway. He's throwin stuff down an makin commando signals. Septic can't make a head or a tail out them but he signals back. Mackenzie can't make a head or a tail out Septic's either. But he keeps on doin it an Septic keeps on doin it back an catchin boxes an stackin them in the trolley.

I'm sure I can see Septic droolin at the sweeties. It's these silver lines down his chin. Sometimes they're yella in the lights. There's fags too, an other boxes. I can't see what they are. It's the last box. Next thing SAS Mackenzie parashoots onto the grass. I knew how to do that too ma da showed me. Off the sideboard. I showed Gal off the electricity boxes. I don't know if Gal showed anybody. Mibbi I'll ask him. Septic's inspectin some packets of stuff. Mackenzie grabs them off him. That's how I knew what it was cos Septic goes, *What ye nickin the stockins for?* An Mackenzie draws him daggers – *Shut it,* he goes. He must want the stockins for Big Wilma Mackenzie.

When they start wheelin the trolley it skweeks like a million mouses at cheese time. Even I jump back. Sonny Hammil must be deaf. They stop dead. Ye can see Septic an

Mackenzie arguin. The moon comes out purple clouds. Ye can see the Peak changin colour. One minute it's grey next thing it's blue. An the street looks blue. The trolley's shinin an there's two black shapes mumblin. It's like a Walt Disney.

Anyway. Might be mad but he's no daft Mackenzie. He says somethin to Septic an they lift the trolley an carry it down the street an round the corner. They're body snatchers. There's this silence – the kind that's so quiet ye just know there's somethin goin on. Then Skweek

an disappearin out into the distance.

They're all in the kitchen watchin Randall an Hopkirk drinkin ginger an eatin pan drops an oddies. So I sneaks out the front door. It's dark sept for two circles of light at the lampies. I could hear ma feetprints comin back down the lane at me. Me an Gal's got a new signal. I throws a dod of muck on his room an he pops up right away. It's the outline ye can see. The only other ears it could be was his Pluff an he's up the Berries.

The dod of muck's slidin down the glass still when Gal zoooooooooooooooooooooooooooooooooooooooooooooooooooooms

in the garden. He's eatin an outsider on sausage. Square.
Tomato sauce's dribblin down his chin. I points an he flicks
his bready tongue out an licks it like a lizard.

Ma da's drunk. Sleepin. Slid this right out his hand. He breaks
me a bit off an I stuffs it in ma mouth. Bad idea cos then I
couldn't tell him about Sonny Hammil's van. So I gives it the
nod that means I'm goin to tell ye somethin great soon as
I've finished this. What ye do is ye chew an chew an make
yer eyes wide an point at the thing ye're eatin noddin yer
head forward about once every second. I'm chewin like a
mad dog all the way up the lane.

It's nearly Wine Alley when there's enough room for
bread an words. I tell Gal all about Mackenzie an Septic. Gal
listens like a rabbit. He could listen like nothin on earth. I
liked watchin him listenin for trains an stuff so I did. I'd
shake ma head blowin air out ma mouth. If anybody passed
an looked when he was stood like a statue I'd open ma eyes
right wide an say, *He's listenin.* They always lower their
eyebrows an walk away as if we stole their washin.

Skweek skweek skweek skweek

Skweek skweek skweek skweek

Skweek skweek skweek skweek

Skweek skweek skweek skweek

Skweek skweek skweek skweek

Skweek skweek skweek skweek

Skweek skweek skweek skweek

SHIT! We nearly bump right into Mackenzie an Septic.
Before they see us we've crashed through Munchie's back
hedges.

C'mon! goes Gal an rolls an runs an rolls through
Munchie's back into their front. Ziggin an zaggin. They've

got to go by Munchie's front to get out Wine Alley –
Mackenzie an Septic.

Soon as we poke out the front hedges this drunk wummin
starts skelpin Gal's face wi a fish supper. Howlin like a
banshee. Gal near ripped his ears off gettin back. He's holdin
his ears an screamin wi no noise. Lookin right at me. Ma
soldiers're sniggerin but he can't see them. The wummin's got
one of them dogs that barks for Scotland. Shortbread tin dogs
they're called. I think. Sonny Hammil's got one an it chases ye
out the lane gnashin at yer ankles. It's sore. But Sonny
Hammil watches from the scullery an does ye in if ye kick it.

This other night what does the bold Gal do? Does he not
just turn the corner an scream like it's sank the gnashers in
sore. *ARGH GH GH GH GH* he's goin like in the
comics. Sonny Hammil smiles an sticks the chip pan on. Or
toast an cheese.

But what Gal really does is spin soon as he's round the
corner an hits it a almighty kick screamin so ye can't hear its
yelps. So when Sonny Hammil sees it runnin back barkin
like the street's on fire he thinks it's took a lump out Gal.

He thinks it's sayin, *Hey see that Sonny! I just took a lump
out his leg there.*

But what it's really sayin is, *Hey you ya big baldy bastard he
put the boot right in ma ribs there – a Gallacher too!! Did ye not
hear me yelpin!!??*

Sonny Hammil never liked them since Jim Gal burnt his
back shed down.

Anyway. *Woof woof* this dog's goin an the wummin's
draggin it along the street. I knew Gal wanted to give the
wummin the treatment. But there was two things we never
wanted.

1   Mackenzie to see us.

The other thing we never wanted was:

2   The wummin to do us in.

Nothin worse than a drunk wummin. *I've more scars off drunk wimmin than Germans,* ma granada used to say. He was in the War.

The dog's barkin at passin cars. Then here comes skweek skweek skweek skweek. Me an Gal wait for a bit an then vault the fence an walk dead ordinary. We were great at that me an Gal – vaultin fences an walkin dead ordinary. It was like we materialised in mid-walk. Like the Invisible Man an his pal an some eejit switches the wrong plasma switch an there we are walkin down the street. All of a suddenly.

Mackenzie's shovin the trolley past these aul wimmin at the bus stop. They all swing their heads like tennis. Nastase he's great. Me an Gal love him. *Hello Mrs Kelly. Hello Mrs Brown,* Septic's goin wi a big daft grin. But all Mrs Brown an Mrs Kelly can say is *Tut tut tut,* an this other wummin's pointin her nose up like she's tryin to see through her nostrils.

There's all these trees behind the bus stop. Gal looks at me – I looks at him. They're goin down the Valley.

Guess what? We're zooooooooooooooooooooooooooooooomin across the road an this Polis car nearly kills us. We fling ourselfs on the kerb spectin the aul wimmin to be amazin.

Isn't it a miracle they're not dead Sadie?

Aye Jeannie – phone Sister Mary Brigitte get her down here wi the rosary beads.

But they don't. So we stop holdin each other up an doin can't breathe. They're watchin the Polis car the wimmin. An Mackenzie's watchin the Polis car. Septic's pushin the trolley faster an faster. His bony elbows're stickin up the hill at us. When he turns his head he looks like he's walkin towards us but gettin further away. The Polis's big draft board foreheads're turnin as they pass. Mackenzie hides his face. The wimmin're smilin an foldin their arms. Waitin. They look like the big fat wummin on Tom an Jerry that stands wi her arms folded tap tappin her toes.

But the Polis go right past Mackenzie so the wimmin unfold the arms an start goin on like the bus droove right by them wi the driver hangin out singin Gary Glitter. ♪ *Doo doo doo doo doooo I love you love...my only true love...*

Mackenzie's always doin us in an takin our money an frogs but I don't even want him caught. Ye'd think I'd go right up there an say,

Excuse me wimmin at the bus stop but I know where he's goin wi that stuff I think we should phone the Polis.

But I don't really like the wimmin. Gal's the same. He's watchin the Polis car like we're on the run. Like it's goin to come an stick us in Tom Dunnachie's home. Or the Mary's.

But then the brake lights come on like a good second idea. They start turnin. But they're no good. They hit the wheels off one kerb then the other. They do it a million times. It's like it's a game they're playin. Hit The Kerb As Many Times As Ye Can. Even I know a three-point turn. Gal's big brothers know everythin about cars. They can spot what kind it is away down on the Old Monkland Road – an that's from the Lane at Cadzow. They know all about three-point turns, emergency stops, skids, handbrake turns. A three-point turn's when ye turn a car an ye've got to touch the kerb three times sactly an the third time yer motor's pointin the other way from the way it was pointin the last time ye looked.

Mackenzie knew about turns an all. He does a one-point turn into the bushes. The wimmin're too busy smilin an turnin their noses up an suckin in big lumps of air. Mackenzie an Septic heave the trolley in the trees in a oner. Nobody sees it. Not the Polis. Not the Bus Stop. Only me an Gal.

The Polis car comes back lookin left an right. They'd be as well doin somersaults an tap dancin wi the siren an wee blue light cos once ye're in the Valley there's no findin ye.

A right laugh so it is. The wimmin take their eyes off the Polis to look at Mackenzie an he's not there. It's like a magic trick. They're the same surprised as if one of them just varnished in the air an all that's left is her twenty-four-hour bra. Playtex. *Best thing on the Telly,* Gal says. Alla kazam poof an she's gone. An this Playtex slaps off the ground.

Mackenzie's gone. They're all lookin about for whose fault it is.

 It's ours. Me an Gal. They grab us.

Right it's the Polis for youse, they're goin. *Youse're in that Mackenzie gang.*

Yer hands off me, says Gal usin his wriggle-out move. He's the other side of me before ye can say Magic Roundabout. But the witches're not for lettin me go. They're all round me. It's all big bulgin bloodshot eyes an tombstone teeth. Their breath's stinkin. Oozin out gaps in their teeth like rotten porridge. An these big jaggy noses're pokin in ma face. It's like they've stuck toilet brushes up their nostrils. An there's this smell of pish.

I know your mother, an all this they're sayin. But they're liars cos if they know yer maw they always go, *You're Alice Riley's laddie — I'll be tellin her at the bingo themorra night.*

Gal shouts *LOOK, A SUBMARINE!!!* an rips me away when they turn their heads. By this time the Polis car's away up the street scratchin its head. The wimmin fold their arms an complain.

When the Polis car is two wee pin-size red lights at the Woodside Gal nudges me. The wimmin're statues an I laugh. But he gives me the *no not the wimmin* nudge an nods at the trees. The rosiedendrons're movin. Next thing this trolley comes firin out. It's like there's a trolley launcher in there. First trolley on the moon. Can ye magine it?

Eh Buzz Aldrin here – eh Hoostin – one small step for me – eh Hoostin – eh – there's an ASDA trolley up here!

KERASH it goes on the pavement. The Bus Stop turns round pressin their necks wi one hand an reachin out an pokin each other wi the other hand. Like the trolley's a ghost. It wanders drunk down the pavement goin towards this manhole wi light comin up. The wimmin're watchin an all. Next thing this Workie pops his head up an back down again. He never seen the trolley. The wimmin's eyes get wide but they don't say nothin. They keep starin at the trolley.

An another thing. This right muscley boxer dog's sniffin about. It say's *Oho what's this then? Open manhole – that's handy.* The dog shoves its head down the manhole wi its arse pointin up. Its wee cut-off tail's goin from side to side like a mad upside down pendulum. It's like a cartoon. The trolley whacks the boxer dog in the manhole. There's this quiet bit. The Day The World Stood Still it is. Next thing there's this almighty barkin an shoutin comin out the manhole. The Workie's head appears, then the dog.

The Workie.

The Dog.

Workie.

Dog.

WorkieDogWorkieDogWorkieDogWorkieDogWorkieDog
WorkieDogWorkieDogWorkieDogWorkieDogWorkieDog
WorkieDogWorkieDogWorkieDogWorkieDogWorkieDog
WorkieDogWorkieDogWorkieDog

The wimmin at the bus stop stare. Next thing the one that thinks she's the leader goes *That's… that's terrible that.* An all the other wimmin nod their heads *Aye… Mm Mm… Aye… That's right… Mm Mm…* they're goin an foldin their arms.

Me an Gal snuck in the trees. We hardly make a rattle. The moon's out so the ground's blue an the leafs're black. Well they're not really black they're green but they look black. An plastic. They're shinin like plastic. Except where the moon hits them full on. Then they're silver.

This way, Gal whispers after listenin. We're movin downhill an Septic an Mackenzie's mumblin's comin up through the trees. The dark's tunnelin out in front of us like a giant rabbit hole. There's twigs cracklin an soft thumps of big clumpy Mackenzie feet an wee sneaky Septic feet.

We stop halfway down. Hunkers. There's nothin but the silver burn an the black shape of the Pipe goin over it again an again. An the Peak's stickin up in the distance like a giant fang. Mackenzie's stopped somewhere. Mibbi he heard us? We sat like lumps of wood. We could sit still like anythin. We never even moved our eyes. It was ages. Then there's shapes against the Burn carryin these square things.

C'mon, goes Gal: *time we were makin tracks.* He's runnin really loud I'm thinkin when he shouts back at me to hurry up, *Hurry up Derrick keep up wi ma tracks.*

I starts thinkin Gal's lost his touch. I'm wantin to go on ma hunkers cos Mackenzie's bound to've heard us. He's probably pickin up jaggy rocks.

But he's not daft Gal. *Nobody sept the Champions can hear right next to the Burn,* he tells me later on when I ask him.

KLANG. We're on the Pipe. I'm shufflin along it. I'm

shufflin ma feet an makin ma toes look for the lumpy bits so as I don't fall in. Magine fallin in in the dark? Ye'd be wonderin when ye were goin to hit the bottom.

Gal's up on the concrete bit. Me an Gal used to fight about it all the time. He used to say it was cement an I used to say it was concrete. Anyway we don't fight about that any more. It's daft. We're supposed to be pals us.

Gal's got eyes like a owl. He stares away down the Burn. *There!* he goes. I can see nothin but black an blue an silver. Then I hears somethin. Next thing there's Mackenzie an Septic walkin under the Pipe. We start followin them. Every time they move we move. *C'mon!* Gal goes over his soldier back at me wi his whisper that comes out the side of his mouth. Every time they stop Gal shoves his palms out to the side feelin for two walls that aren't there an we stop dead. Ye can hear Mackenzie an Septic listenin. But they can listen nothin. For ages we're right above them listenin an movin. Movin an listenin. Two wood pigeons flap away. They look great crossin the moon. For a minute I forget I'm balanced on the Pipe. Gal's lookin at them too. Our bodies disappear in the dark an our eyes're far satellites followin the soarin birds across the stars.

The Pipe goes up the Slaggy. We follow them all the way even if it is night. I mind shiverin at the towerin Slaggys. Specially the Peak. They plank the stuff in this hole. I'm lyin flat on the pipe but I can still hear them over the trundlin water inside. Gal's nearly upside down pokin his head down the gap between the Pipe an the concrete bits. If ye fell down there yer head'd get stuck an it'd be a hinge an ye'd swing an swing chokin. If Mackenzie never got ye first.

Mackenzie an Septic go the other way from the way they came in. Gal marks the Pipe wi the heel of his guttie. A black rubber streak. We lie there listenin to their shoutin an laughin meltin in wi the Burn. Till it's lower than the odd bird whistlin. We head back down the Pipe to the Valley.

The Piggery

Next day me an Gal's goin go through the Piggery. But there's no pigs that we've ever seen. They're always doin that yer maw an da – callin things daft names. Like the Piggery wi not a pig in sight – *Not even the odd slice of ham,* Gal says. *Be as well callin it* the King Kongery *cos he's not there either.*

Danishzhzhshshshshshshshshshshshshs, Gal used to say every time I asked him about it.

But Gal wha...?

Danishzhzhshshshshshshshshshshshshs,

Och Gal but how's there no...?

Danishzhzhshshshshshshshshshshshshs, he'd keep on sayin. It was no use talkin to him when he was like that. That was his keep on sayin it mood.

Gal's da STOLE a pig. A real pig – curly tail – four soup hoofs. He never stole it over the Piggery but. Got it down the Jap's farm. The Polis came. CID. It was a laugh.

Reason to believe you have a stolen pig in there Mr Gallacher?

The whole street's out. Spot a CID a mile away. Ma maw's huntin me in an bendin round the doorpost herself.

Hi Yi Mary, she says when Maw Gal sees the edge of her

face, *this doorpost here needs paintin!* Maw Gal draws her daggers an slams the door.

Big Gal goes, *Oshiferr ma ma farm house Pig? Pig ye say?* But by this time the Polis're up the stairs. *I'll take this all the way to the* Sunday Mail, he's shoutin, *The Judge'll be hearin about this.* But the CID're laughin at this big pink pig hangin above the bath. *Neck's slashed open like a purse,* Gal says. *The last of its blood drip drippin in the white bath. Like jelly.*

Gal says every time they get ham Maw Gal chews these wee chews an stares at Big Gal munchin away. She looks at the ham hangin on her fork for a minute an then

shrieeeeeeeeeeeeeeeeeeeeeeeeeeeeeeeeeeeeeeeeeeeeeeeeek
She sets about Big Gal wi the fish lifter. It's cos of

The Coatbridge and Airdrie Advertiser

STOLE A PIG AND AWAY HE RUN

Wi a picture of Big Gal's bristly face below it. Smilin. Like a skinny Desperate Dan.

Smilin ya bastard! Maw Gal'd shout. I've heard her. *I'll give ye smilin – we're the laughin stock,* an she'd chase him out wi the fish lifter. He'd fly out the door wi his hands on his head an his elbows pointin in the air. But he's some man Big Gal cos even if he looks terryfied when he runs out – he always comes back home singin. Gal takes after him. Boldness wise. She's not too happy about another thing too, Maw Gal, cos at the top of the lane it says

DA GAL THE UGLY RUNT STOLE A PIG AND AWAY HE RAN

Don't tell nobody but Gal done it. This red spray paint we found in the British. He sprayed it an this is what I remember about it. I remember he had the same look in his eye he had when he done this thing to Septic. I'm goin to tell ye about that. Same as when he stuck the knife in Strangler Joe's leg that on time. His eyes go all narrow an his mouth turns up like a smile wi no teeth lookin out. *I hate ma da*, he says, *I'd blow him up if I had dynamite, or poison him. Arsenic. I'd put him through Pender's mincer.*

Sometimes his da batters him an Jim jumps in an Pluff an they batter Big Gal. Friday specially. I never thought it bothered Gal that much cos it happens all the time. But this day I asked him about it an he started greetin. I just walked on talkin about eggs an this great swing I found an kiddin in I never noticed. *Ye never know what's goin on in peoples heads,* ma maw always goes. She's right. It's like there's all these wee films projected on the inside of everybody's head. Only them can see it. When ye peek in their eyes ye only see the film that's on the back of their heads. No way they'll let ye in to see the big picture on the front. Hmm! Try gettin in there wi a jam jar. That's what ma da's always goin on about. *When I was your age we got in the Odeon wi a jam jar an still had enough left to feed the whole street wi fish suppers.* That's what him an Doctor Flannagin go on about when Flannagin's in gettin ma da to blow up bags an try to burst them.

Magine it. *Gal here's a jam jar so let's see inside yer skull. Oh an by the way – break a couple of bits of glass off an run down Krick's an get fifteen million fish suppers an send them to Biafra.*

ARGHGHGHGHGHGHGHGH!!!!!!!!!!!!!!!!!!!!!!!!
– That'd be the swift kick I'd get. Christ! what am I on about now? Ma head's away wi it. They should lock me up.

You're head's full of wee motors all bumpin into each other, ma da says. I listen sometimes for the engines. This day I wasn't sure if it was the motors or this purrin cat on the back shed. *Scat cat!* I goes an chucks a plasticine Gigantor.

Anyway. This day we're over the Piggery. Ye go through the Piggery an by Ireland's to get to the Oil Pond. They've got a big machine in Ireland's that eats cars at one end an posts them out the other end the size of a shoe box – PLONK – nice as ye like – square an shiny. *Ye could drive in an walk away wi yer car under yer arm,* Gal says. I says *They're too heavy to lift,* but he says *How can anythin the size of a shoe box be too heavy to lift? I mean we can lift drainer lids an they're iron. Solid.*

He's always tryin to say the opposite these days. This time I says the Earth's goin to die cos it moves closer to the sun.

Quarter an inch a year, I says.

I know, he says, *an that pig ma da stole flew out the toilet windae.*

It's true. It's in a book.

Iiiiiin aaaaaaaa booooooooook!!??

I hated when he made the words so I felt daft. Same as teachers. Like I never read it in a book. Like I made it all up.

I did – a book about space – quarter an inch a year.

He looks at me. But I can tell he's interested even if he's chuckin stones at this washin machine in the Burn.

Will we crash into it? he goes.

No. I catches the sun an the earth an starts bringin them closer thegether.

It'll move like this till it's too hot on this planet to live.

I mind that. He's starin at the earth – ma hand really. An he's seein it all burnt like a tennis ball flung in a fire. That's what's in his eyes. I can see it movin about his blue bits. He's lookin for an answer. He's good at answers like how to get there the quickest an how to stay out Mackenzie's road. An Different Ways. Runnin different ways if anybody chases us. This is the whole planet. But if anybody can get an answer Gal can. He's the man for that.

We walk on worried about burnin up. He's puttin the palm of his hand up to the clouds an feelin it on his face. The third time he looks at me an blows some air out his mouth.

That means it feels hot – the sun. That means he believes me really. So that means the answer's on its way.

It's ages. Then he comes away wi, *Mibbi the sun'll cool down as we're movin towards it?*

I gives him the great answer nod. It's a lot of nods quick, one after the other. Wi a smile an all.

Aye Gal that's it, I'm dead excited cos he looks happier now that we're not gettin frazzled. *That's it an mibbi God'll be washin his Rolls Royce an the water'll splash off it an cool the sun down so as we'll be that close we'll be able to touch it.*

Hand's off that sun now boys. OK God sorry about that big man. I like yer motor but, Gal says wi all these different voices. He's great at different voices Gal. An *vroom vroom* he drives off through the trees wi his Rolls Royce. Gal's great so he is. Hunner per cent. Spot on.

But I was tellin ye about the Oil Pond. Ye go round the back of Ireland's an there's a lane between that an the Woodyard. The Woodyard's millions of logs stacked up for miles. Ye can run over the tops but ye get fed up. They don't move like lumberjack films or nothin. Me an Gal flung some down in the Oil Pond this time an tried walkin on them. We sank.

Ye go down this path an the Oil Pond's at the bottom. There's oil on the surface. It makes rainbows. I was daft when I was young – I used to try an fish the rainbows out. Gal'd be catchin frogs an newts an I'd be up the other end timmin ma net into a jar an starin for the rainbow. Every time I looked it was on the water surface an every time I splashed ma fingers in it wasn't there.

I like pond skaters. They walk over the skim of oil an these wee multi coloured circles appear round their feet. Like they're wearin seekwince on their feet.

It's five thousand feet in the middle. Nobody's ever touched the bottom. It's a crater. *A volcano,* Gal says. The water's warm an there's red in it, an green, an foam, an black oil, an rainbows, an all this other stuff. Even all the ground's rusty.

I'll tell ye what else is there – these big round wooden things for keepin cable on. They float. We use them as rafts. Ye get a big stick out the Widdy an shove it round like gongdolas. But ye always go round the edge. Middle's too deep. Gal says his Jim says a whirlpool's in it an that's what happened to Mad Gary Brannigan. He got sucked down it OK an blew back out mental. Bonkers. He can't even talk right now but he was top of the class before it. He goes to Drumpark now. Grey bus. *Drumchuckie,* Gal calls it.

But this day that I'm talkin about – we're down the Oil Pond – no nets or nothin. Gal's firin his sling at big brown reeds. They're explodin like a bomb wi the sound turned down.

BARRRRRRRRRRRRRRRRRRRRROOOOF

I miss all the time. Even if I fire where there's millions the stone swerves corners to miss.

Ireland's an the Widdy's got a side each of the Oil Pond. It's only got three sides. It's a triangle. The other side's railway. If ye cross the railway ye're in the Slaggy. But me an Gal hardly go there cos Gangs sniff glue an drink an fight wi sords. Pat The Leg – that's what happened to him. He was in the Slaggy. He got chased by the Tamla Hill an he got ran over wi a train. That's how he's only got one leg now – an that's sewed on.

The railway's the border. I always feel safe down the Oil Pond even if it is deep as Loch Ness. I get feart even lookin up over the railway at the Peak stickin up on its own – higher than all the other Slaggy Hills. It's watchin ye. But that's daft – who ever heard of a hill wi eyes?

Gal's loadin his sling wi wee round railway stones. I always get some an keep them secret till he runs out away miles from any railway an then I go,

Ah ha! An whip them out ma pocket. He always lights up an takes one out ma palm like it's a diamond an makes the best shot of the day.

BARRRRRRRRRRRRRRRRRRRROOOOF

He explodes another one.

Troops out!

Eh?

Troops out – that's what ma da shouts.

How.

Ireland.

I look up at Ireland's car eatin machine. Sometimes I don't know what he's on about.

Sometimes I don't know what you're on about Gal.

I does the waitin for an answer look. It's hands on yer hips an the head tilted. Oh! – an yer mouth hangin open.

Ireland – the country! he goes like he's fed up already talkin about it.

That reminds me. See how I was on about ma maw an da callin things stupit names? Well another thing's puzzlin me too. Yup. Definitely puzzlin me.

They're always goin on about Ireland. Everybody. I gets this map out spectin it to be up past Airdrie. It's miles away!! There's sea an everythin. It's this big island. Ireland! Island! Should've guessed.

An Priests – they're all Irish. Weird. Mibbi they can't get jobs in Ireland. Even ma maw an da go on about it. Ma granny – she's worse. Oh – before I forget – there's this street called Sunnyside. It looks alright when it's sunny. But what about when it's rainin?

It's all mixin me up too much. That's how I like just me an Gal at the Oil Pond not talkin. Just sittin. Just him firin the sling when he feels like it an turnin to me grinnin. An the sun makin magic splinters on the water. I love the noise the stones make when they sploosh in. An then it's quiet an these ripples rucklin up under the rainbow an shovin out quiet to the edges. Inches below the surface these frogs're doin breast strokes through cold water keepin up wi the rainbow's edge. An below them – dark. I don't know what it is but I keep thinkin that's where ye go when ye die. Brrrrr. It sends ice through me. When I shake the thought off an think of good things Gal's sittin wi his knees up an droppin stones in the water. Fed up. I know he's fed up.

I'm fed up, he goes an PLOP another stone bursts the rainbow, leavin a wee black pool closin in to a dot.

See! I knew he was fed up.

What about Mackenzie's swedgers? I goes. I don't know why I sayed that. I wasn't even thinkin about them at the time. I was in a wee ship like the Whizzers of Oz've got in the Topper an I was curvin through the tops of the reeds an a big meteorite comes burnin past. That'd be Gal an his sling – but it's dreamin so it can be anythin. But anyway I wasn't thinkin about Mackenzie so I don't know how I sayed it. I wish I never now.

Gal looks like I asked him to derail a train. Or blow up the world. Or smash a whole nest of swan's eggs wi a boat rower.

They're over the Slaggy in that hole. You marked the Pipe wi yer guttie. We could just take some.

There I go again. Sayin things I don't even mean.

Off of Mackenzie?

He says that like I've sayed, *Let's go in the Woodside an stick some knittin needles through your da's head.* Even thinkin about Mackenzie gives me the shakers. Usually.

Go in the Slaggy then.

Gal whips round. His sling's hangin at his side an a stone rolls slow out the leather cradle. *The Slaggy!!? Ye mental!!?? That's where he'll be!* He picks the stone up an fires it in the Slaggy.

We could just look? I goes.

Gal looks up at the railway. I look at him. He does his I'll do it but I know we're goin to get into trouble headshake an crunches up the steep hill.

Galderrick

Gal's walkin on a rail an flappin his wings up an down like a chicken an I'm on one leg hoppin. It's not easy. Hoppin. Ye've got to hold one leg up yer back wi yer other hand that's not out balancin ye up.

So he's flappin an I'm on one leg. But that's not all – we're sactly in time. We're a machine. A GALDERRICK that's what kind we are. Two of them wee fellas in Swish clocks that come out an dance all over the place every half hour. We're like them cos every time I hop Gal's wings go up an every time I hop again they go down. But that's all. It's usually a wee log cabin an trees an nice curtains an stuff on them Swish clocks. I mean I've never seen one of them clocks wi a Railway an an Oil Pond an the Slaggy on it. But that's what a GALDERRICK clock'd be like.

I'm doin zippy-zoom laser beam eyes for the Tecs cos there's millions of railways at this bit an they can come from anywhere so they can. Gal pulls the sling out. I *member* sact cos I spots this Pale Ale tin miles down the tracks wi ma

laser beams. I starts singin ♪*Mecewans is the best buy the best*

buy the best buy, Mecewans is the best buy, the best buy in beer. Hey Mecewans...

WshshshPING!!!!!!!

The can leaps up doin silent somersaults an falls an there's Gal grinnin wi his sling in his hand. An then there's a clang. Gal's lips're doin the sact same curve the sling's doin. Gal'd be a great gunslinger. I've always sayed that.

You'd be a great gunslinger Gal so ye would. I used to always go an he'd blow smoke off the top of his sling an spin it round his finger an shove it in his pocket like John Wayne.

Gerr outa town, he'd go an start runnin. *Yee ha! Awday Gallacher's comin at yees ya smelly fuckers.*

Swearin all the time now Gal. More than ten times a day. At least. That's when I thought I seen somethin in the trees. Somethin reflectin on the white shiny bits the sun makes on the top of the leaves. An movin. Movin sideways keepin up wi us. I was always on the lookout after Strangler Joe tried to drag us in the trees.

Gal d'you believe in Cyclepaths? I goes.

But he ignores me.

There's a Cyclepath escaped out Carstairs. Muddered six wee boys when ma da was wee. Chopped them all up. In bits.

Gal gives me a right Yar look.

He made the best Meccano stuff ye ever seen. Showed ye on the Telly. All brammers Gal – pure brammers. Big cranes an boats an an aeroplane – wi a propeller – Meccano six Gal – the one wi the motor in it – an the plane can fly.

Gal stops skwintin out his eyes like the Muttley dog an I know he's ready to do the laugh so I goes dead loud an fast

HeusedtotricktheweeboysinwiththeMeccannoankil lthemanchopthemup!

Hee hee hee hee rassin fassin rassin fassin...

See! I knew he was goin to laugh.

I stuck ma chin up in the air. I stuck ma chin up in the air for two reasons.

1   It made him mad.

2   It looks like I'm not carin.

Meccano Joe – that's his name, I goes. But Gal fell off the track laughin. He looks round pushin his belly up an down wi the palms of his hands.

Meccano Joe!???

Then he looks up the sky like him an God's best pals.

You made that up!

That was it. I puts ma chin on ma chest an storms off in the huff. I'm great at that – puttin ma chin so ye know I'm in the huff.

I always march away wi ma legs straight when I'm in the huff an I fire the elbows out to side when I'm walkin – I got that off a cartoon. Daffy the Duck. Sometimes I'd go Ha ha ha haaa ha but hardly ever.

Gal's shoutin the odds but he doesn't even knock me out ma march even a wee bit. His words're skelpin ma back an whizzin round ma side an floatin away down the tracks. Like they're a river an I'm this rock.

Meccano Joe – Hmph. I'd be keepin a sharp lookout for the Bricklayer if I was you. An Mackenzie.

His words're rebouncin off everywhere now. I'd've never've stopped. I'd've walked to America. There's trains go from here to America. Me an Gal's goin to get food an hide in one. They go to Holytown – that's where they make films. Gal says Big John Wayne'd put us up for a couple of nights no problem. This Buckie bottle explodes right in ma face nearly. I dove in the grass spectin Gal to come runnin to the rescue but all he can do is laugh. His laughin's gettin sliced up by the grass. I'm turnin ma head real slow in case it's a madman wi a sluggie an there's Gal blowin the smoke off his sling.

Eat dirt ya sonofabitch, he goes. Ye've got to laugh. That's what ma maw says when Gal's givin her some lip.

But it reminded me of this time I got shot. It was just after Strangler Joe. Me an Gal'd stopped goin up the Lochs. This night we're down the Gravy. There's this bit an the graves've got skulls n crossbows on them. Thousand years old. A least. There's this tomb an if ye go down by the third step ye go missin. They've blocked it up wi stones now.

Me an Gal's pokin sticks in the gaps tryin to make the tips go missin. But ye've probably got to walk in at midnight an say the Our Father backwards or somethin.

SCHWIIIIIIIIIIIIIIIIIIIIIIIIIIIIIIIIIIIIIIIIIIIIISH

PHUTTTT

I looks up an Gal's zig zaggin through the gravestones shoutin.

RUN DERRICK RUN LIKE FUCK!!!

I starts runnin. I don't know what it is.

SCHWIIIIIIIIIIIIIIIIIIIIIIIIIIIIIIIIIIIIIIIIIIIIIIISH

PHUTTT

I starts ziggin through the gravestones an all. When Gal's zaggin I'm ziggin an when he's ziggin I'm zaggin. I'm only ziggin cos I can see him zaggin. I still don't know what it is.

SCHWIIIIIIIIIIIIIIIIIIIIIIIIIIIIIIIIIIIIIIIIIIIIIISH

Gal vaults the wall an it's just his hands an his head shoutin louder. I'm still zoomin through the stones. But I'm ziggin too much an gettin further away from Gal an the wall. I'm not zaggin enough.

ZAG!! ZAG LIKE FUCK!!

I starts zaggin like fuck.

SCHWIIIIIIIIIIIIIIIIIIIIIIIIIIIIIIIIIIIIIIIIIIIIIISH

PHUTTT

I'm feet from the wall an Gal's eyes're doin big magnets an draggin me faster. We're touchin distance an,

SCHWIIIIIIIIIIIIIIIIIIIIIIIIIIIIIIIIIIIIIIIIIISHS ACKACKACKACKACKACKACKACKACKA

The world's all white. That's all it is. This white an spinnin an pain pain pain.

Next thing ma face scraped down a stone. Past the skull an crossbows an I'm decked. Somethin's scudded ma back. Sore. Like gettin a boot on the back but mixed in wi whacked wi a palin on the head too.

Get behind that gravestone, Gal shouts. *BELLYFLAP!! BELLYFLAP!!*

I drag maself over an Gal disappears. All I can hear is his muffled voice shoutin to stay down , stay down an,

SCHWIIIIIIIIIIIIIIIIIIIIIIIIIIIIIIIIIIIIIIIIIISH PING

SCHWIIIIIIIIIIIIIIIIIIIIIIIIIIIIIIIIIIIIIIIIIISH PING

SCHWIIIIIIIIIIIIIIIIIIIIIIIIIIIIIIIIIIIIIIIIIISH PING

SCHWIIIIIIIIIIIIIIIIIIIIIIIIIIIIIIIIIIIIIIIIIIISH PING

I'm crushed up to Andrew Smith, 1823 – 1904. The letters were printed on ma head in mirror language. Anyway, the noise stops an Gal limps me up the road. I'm roarin. Gal doesn't say nothin. Most other guys'd slag ye rotten. But not him. Not the bold Gal. No sir. He's got his arm round like it's the war an we're wounded. It reminded me of Rolf Harris an the two boys that've only got one horse an the two of them go on it an then they're in a war an this one's lyin wounded an the other one goes up an gets him an sings

Did ye think I would leave you dyin when there's room on ma horse for two. It's good. Me an Gal sing it. 'Long haired Lover From Liverpool'. Gal loves that too. He's great at Jimmy Osmond.

It was Mackenzie wi his sluggie *A Webley Hawk,* Gal says, *Two o two. Thirty quid out Gibsons.* That's what got me on the back. I've still got the hole. Ye can put a match right in it. *Aye a Celtic Match,* Gal always says when I say that.

We're not grasses or anythin but, *It's a gun,* Gal says. *Could've been dead.* So we goes round to Mackenzie's. He's not in but Gal lifts ma jumper an shows Big Wilma the hole in ma back. She's fumin. There's steam comin out her eyes. Next minute ma heart's in ma mouth cos Mackenzie swaggers round the corner wi the gun slung over his soldier. He draws us a look an spits on the ground.

Whit yees doin at ma bit? he says pressin his face on Gal's. Gal swallows a big lump of nothin.

GI ULP!

Let me see yer gun son, says Big Wilma dead nice.
Mackenzie hands her the rifle, still pressin his face on Gal's. He gives it to her backwards an out to the side a bit.

YEARGHRGHRG, she says

an smashes it over his back. She lays right into him till the gun's broke. He's in a ball an moanin. When she's finished she puts a couple of boots in. Me an Gal's quite happy. I'm thinkin she's just about to invite us in for tea when she folds her arms like we're next. She butters pieces up the Rigs, Big Wilma.

Well thanks a lot Mrs Mackenzie. Eh see ye after. Eh...eh...,

We walked out her gate backwards. Mackenzie's bloodshot eyes're glarin through a crack in the fence like a demented cat. Runnin up the street I could hear the boot goin into Mackenzie.

That's it – I'm tellin your social worker, she's screamin. An she must've cos next minute he's in the Mary's.

Blood Brothers
an the Big Yella

It's the same day as the Oil Pond. We're finished lookin into the Slaggy. We're lyin. Head on one track – feet on the other – opposite each other. Comfy. Lookin at the sky – amazin. It was the same feelin as bein in a chapel on yer own when it's rainin only times a million.

I'm right into amazin. I'm always bein amazed at more things than Gal's amazed at. This day I'm amazin at the clouds. They're elephants an even a big Gary Glitter. *CAAAAAA MON! CAAA MON! CAAAAAA MON! CAAA MON! I SAY!!* I goes. Gal ignores me.

Gal, Gary Glitter, I goes, an points wi ma eyebrows. But all he can say is *Where? Where? Where?* till the cloud fades an changes into this big laughin skull. *Ha ha ha,* it's sayin in blue sky cloud language. *Deaththththth!*

We just lie there an it's great. Ye can hear cars on the road an Dundyvan Steelworks clangin. An the Car Eatin Machine. Sometimes a whistlin bird glides along the tracks chirpin. Then it sees Gal an me an veers downhill into the moonrock surface of the Slaggy. Like it's sayin, *Oh aye this is a right peaceful wee flight. I know!! I'll just fly along these silver lines an stay out the road of they human things –* **Jeee sus** there's two *lyin waitin – they're goin to grab me – I know!! I'll veer right an down into the Slaggy even if Mackenzie is down there wi his gang.*

Mackenzie sets fire to nests wi the yunks in them. The yunks think *Oh aye – here's a feed comin* an WHOOSH there's this match that's like a telegraph pole wi flames comin out it. The last thing they see is the flames curvin round Mackenzie's eyeballs. Evil. Like the inside of his head's all flames.

Shhh! Gal goes sittin up sudden. He spits on the track an gets the ear on it. Gal's lugs look bigger these days. Its edges're hangin over the side of the track now. Like a gammon steak. I think his ears're growin faster than his head. If he goes on like this he'll be Plug out the *Beano*'s twin brother.

He listens. There's voices mixin wi birds an stuff. He stands up an says like he's really really sure – *Bricklayer.*

I'm froze. No wonder after the last time. The fastest brick last time knocked this big straight line in the forest an splashed in the Burn an made a ten feet crater under the water. Ye can't really see it now it was ages ago an the trees've grew back an the water's too boggin to see through.

Gal gets back down. He wanted to be really really really sure cos that's what he always wanted to be – really really really sure. If he was just really really sure we'd not know what to do.

Yup! he goes, *Bricklayer,* so he's really really really sure.

Jesus Gal! I always say that when it's somethin bad.

I'm shakin ma head. Whoever heard of anybody gettin caught wi the Bricklayer twice in their lifes? It made me feel famous.

A Fortyer, goes Gal standin up again.

I'm lookin this way an that way. An I'm still lookin the other ways for the Tecs an Mackenzie. An that Cyclepath on the News. Ma head's spinnin wi lookin an I still don't know what's left an what's right on the railway so I don't know what way the train's comin.

Know what? says Gal.

What?

He nods at the Slaggy. It's the Lofty Peak flour advert. The Burn runs through it an beneath the trees underground tunnels go for miles. If ye go in the Echo Tunnel for two weeks ye come out in America. New York. Right under Ireland on the way. Ye need a torch.

Anyway he nods an goes – *C'mon, we'll hide in there this time.* That's sendin me shivers same as the Bricklayer. The reason Gal wanted to go in the Slaggy instead of back down the Oil Pond is the Bricklayer could've nailed us for sure down the Oil Pond. It's just a big hole in the ground really. He'd pick us off. Coconuts we'd be – at the Shows.

Doo door a loo – Custard's last stand an all that's left is Derrick an the bold Gal – sorry there goes a brick right through Gal's face an oops Derrick's a gonner now too it's just stupit lookin Custard swishin his sord about an well I spoke too soon there Custard's head's just stoved in too. Th- th- th- that's all folks.

We've only been in the Slaggy on top of the Pipe watchin Mackenzie last night. But that doesn't count ye've got to put yer feet on the ground. Like Neil Armstrong. But that was all nighttime stuff. This was broad daylight. Gal's big brothers're even feart in there unless they've mibbi got a bottle of Buckie an a palin.

Just to look gallus I picks up this stone an flings it high over the trees into the Slaggy. I'm watchin it an Gal tugs ma sleeve. He tugs it three times sactly. Then twice. I knew there was somethin wrong. The stone's wurrin over the white peaks that's pokin into the sky like big ripped bits of paper. I turns an there it is. It's the size of the High Flats an it's comin at us. It's amazin we can't hear a thing. It's just the usual noisy quiet but we can't hear the train. Nothin. It's a Big

Yella an it's on the track we're on. Gal dove in the tees an I'm in mid-air before he bellyflapps on the ground.

We still can't hear it. *Somethin to do wi the wind,* Gal says. *Geronimo couldn't've heard it,* he says. But that stone that I was on about. That stone that seems like ages ago. Well it's not. It's hardly even a second an it's fallin into the big ripped up bits of paper hills an I hears this scream like,

OOH YA BASTARD!!

An then **the noise of the Big Yella** appeared like somebody just put money in the meter an the telly was left on. Loud.

Gal runs. The train's gettin louder an louder an we're goin down an down into the Slaggy. I'm droppin now an then an so's Gal in case we get our head's stoved in.

The train's made everythin dark but there's still no bricks. I can see its shadow projected on the white hills. A black an white film. A horror. The shadow's movin in an out the bends an shapes of the hills like a mad flat ribbon.

Ye'd think I'd be OK that there's no bricks. But we're still runnin an I'm scareder than if there was bricks cos I'm thinkin the Bricklayer's got a good aim on an any minute this brick's goin to send ma head tumblin into the Burn. Ye'd still be alive it says on the telly this night. Yer brain's still got oxygin. Ye can see an taste an everythin. I'm thinkin I'm goin to be in the Burn wi green slime stickin on ma face an sticklebacks flickin in an out ma mouth. An rats comin at ma eyes. I'd rather have the bricks now. I hate waitin. Hate it.

We're crashin through the trees. The slope's that steep we couldn't stop if we wanted. I'm right behind Gal an the branches're whippin off ma face. I've got ma elbows pointed forwards. We're gettin faster an faster. Ma legs're goin that fast fallin's the next thing. But that's not it. Next thing is we bolt into this clearin an here's Mackenzie an his gang round a fire. Ye'd think they'd kill us right away but they don't. They get up an run a couple of steps cos we're comin at them full force. But after a step an a half they see it's just me an Gal. A pair of diddywashers. Twadgers. They turn back an come at us an we **wumph** right into them. So they get us down an lay the boot in. Me an Gal's curlin up wi our arms over our heads. That's what ye do so they're just bootin yer back an yer legs. It's all these loud thuds an big flashes of light. Like gettin yer photie took.

There's this bit where me an Gal's face to face.

Gal, I goes through ma forearms. *Gaaaaaal!*

His eyes're lightin up wi every kick. There's bangers goin off inside his head.

Alf Tupper Tough of the Track, he says, gruntin like last words. I don't know why but I felt happy at that. None of the kicks were sore any more.

Billy Whizz – right at his back. Gal – Billy... ooff!!!
Mackenzie cracks me one wi his steelies.

The train's goin away an I starts to faint an all these funny things're goin in ma head. I'm on this big white sheet of cardboard – like the stuff ye get at Art. It's just me an Gal. But he's not right. He's not Bold. He's got his head hangin down. Know what he's like? Know they things that're all held thegether wi elastics – wee men, clowns an stuff, an they stand up straight till ye push the bottom in an they go all floppy? That's what he's like. But not like the button's been pushed right in. He's like it's just been pushed a bit an he's ashamed. Like when ye've got to tell the priest about what ye think about.

And when you are in the bath Derrick do you wash yerself?

What a stupit question. What ye supposed to do in the bath – play cricket?

Aye – I mean, Yes Father.

And do you – ahem – wash – ahem – down there?

An then I know what he's gettin at – it's not the floor he's talkin about.

Yes Father.

Well you should spend ten seconds only washing down there.

But he sayed **down there** so as I know he means ma willie.

Right Father. Yes Father, I goes an he fires out the Hail Mary's an Our Fathers. Penats.

There I go again ma head's always runnin away wi me so it is. It'll get me hung one day ma maw says.

Your daydreamin'll get ye hung one day. SALAP!!!

That was for pourin her a cup of tea. Only I was daydreamin so I poured the whole teapot in her cup all over the table an she'd put these doilies out for her knittin bee.

Anyway – see me? I don't know? Gal's on this big sheet of cardboard an he's hangin his head like a dog wi a sausage in its mouth. Caught in the scullery. I can see him but he can't see me. This voice is bellowin out. It's The Wizard of OZ.

You Gallacher are accused of not being no good any more at guessing when the Bricklayer is coming.

Gal twists his toe into the cardboard like a wee lassie.

Have you anything to say? The voice vibrates through his whole body an mine.

Gal shakes his head an his elastic gets slacker.

Nothing!!!!!? The voice says

like sayin nothin's the worst thing he could've sayed.

Gal droops a bit more an I'm thinkin he's goin to keep on droopin till he's just this big droop – like an upside down comma on the white card.

You told Derrick Daniel Riley that the Bricklayer was coming when he wasn't.

Yes.

Have you any explanation?

I thought...

You thought!...You thought! You know what thought done – pished the bed and blamed it on the blankets, the voice says an laughs like a teacher.

I've never seen Gal defeated. The voice is laughin an Gal turns so he's facin sactly away from it. I thinks he's gave up. But no. Not him. Not the Bold Gal. No Sir, he whips the strides down an points his arse at the voice an farts this hurricane fart:

whhhhhhhhhhhhhhhhhhhhhhhhhhhhishshshst

The voice staggers away coughin an splutterin. I run onto the cardboard an Gal sees me. He whips the trousers up an winks.

Next thing this spinnin green thing comes at me wi all these voices. There's flames in it an it gets bigger an bigger.

Mackenzie's gang's all round us an me an Gal's tied thegether back to back an Kenny Grant's got a shite on a stick an he's usin it as smellin salts. *YEEUCH!!!* I folds Gal over pressin away from it. They all point an laugh.

No Bricklayer, I says to Gal.

Shut it Riley, goes Septic.

I feel Gal shruggin the soldiers like he couldn't understand it either.

Me an Gal can talk to each other wi just our soldiers, I'm thinkin when this shiver runs down ma back cos there's Mackenzie on his hunkers at the Burn. He's leanin over the water. I can see his reflection on the movin surface. Hammer

House of Horror. Like his face is meltin. 𝕯𝖗𝖆𝖈𝖚𝖑𝖆. 𝕱𝖗𝖆𝖓𝖐𝖊𝖓𝖘𝖙𝖊𝖎𝖓. 𝖂𝖔𝖑𝖋𝖒𝖆𝖓. 𝕭𝖗𝖎𝖉𝖊 𝖔𝖋 𝕯𝖗𝖆𝖈𝖚𝖑𝖆. 𝕭𝖗𝖎𝖉𝖊 𝖔𝖋 𝕱𝖗𝖆𝖓𝖐𝖊𝖓𝖘𝖙𝖊𝖎𝖓. 𝕭𝖗𝖎𝖉𝖊 𝖔𝖋 𝖙𝖍𝖊 𝖂𝖔𝖑𝖋𝖒𝖆𝖓. 𝕯𝖗𝖆𝖈𝖚𝖑𝖆 𝖆𝖓 𝕱𝖗𝖆𝖓𝖐𝖊𝖓𝖘𝖙𝖊𝖎𝖓. 𝕯𝖗𝖆𝖈𝖚𝖑𝖆 𝖆𝖓 𝖙𝖍𝖊 𝖂𝖔𝖑𝖋𝖒𝖆𝖓. 𝕱𝖗𝖆𝖓𝖐𝖊𝖓𝖘𝖙𝖊𝖎𝖓 𝖆𝖓 𝖙𝖍𝖊 𝖂𝖔𝖑𝖋𝖒𝖆𝖓. 𝕯𝖗𝖆𝖈𝖚𝖑𝖆 𝖆𝖓 𝖙𝖍𝖊 𝕭𝖗𝖎𝖉𝖊 𝖔𝖋 𝕱𝖗𝖆𝖓𝖐𝖊𝖓𝖘𝖙𝖊𝖎𝖓 𝖆𝖓 𝕸𝖆𝖈𝖐𝖊𝖓𝖟𝖎𝖊 𝖆𝖓 𝕸𝖆𝖈𝖐𝖊𝖓𝖟𝖎𝖊. 𝕸𝖆𝖈𝖐𝖊𝖓𝖟𝖎𝖊 𝖆𝖓 𝖙𝖍𝖊 𝖂𝖔𝖑𝖋𝖒𝖆𝖓. 𝕸𝖆𝖈𝖐𝖊𝖓𝖟𝖎𝖊 𝖊𝖆𝖙𝖘 𝖙𝖍𝖊 𝖂𝖔𝖑𝖋𝖒𝖆𝖓.

Gal talks wi his soldiers again. It's Septic. He's comin at us wi a burnin stick. Another horrible thing is there's this rabbit on a stick roastin over the fire. Its fur's burnin. It's ears're still movin. Swear! It's wee fluffy tail's throbbin wi fear.

Septic's head's got blood on it. So's the back of his hand. There's this red smudge where it's been tricklin down.

Youse chuck a stone? he goes.

The backs of me an Gal's heads clack off each other as we're noddin.

Yees did!

He shoves the burnin stick right up at me an I can smell ma singed hair. He's face to face an I'm thinkin I've got a parrot on ma soldier cos he's got some skwint. *He's got one eye comin home wi the chips an the other one on a rocket to the moon,* Gal says stuff like that about him all the time.

Septic's sookin up a slabber off his chin. I'm tryin not to laugh. Gal's soldiers start tryin not to laugh like chapel. But that's a laugh, Septic an alter boy an Mackenzie a Priest.

Good mornin Faaa-ther Maaackenzieieiei, the wanes'd go at school – right yar!

Mackenzie's got somethin under the water. I'm thinkin it's a fish mibbi. But there's no fish. They're all dead wi plooshin out Kirk Chemicals an Dundyvan. Sticklebacks just. *They could live down a shitty toilet them,* Gal says. So it might be a body. Somethin he's just kilt. Like another rabbit. The rabbit's stopped movin an its juices're drippin in the fire, sizzlin. That saves us cos Septic goes an strokes up the fire. He's makin sure the gang know it's his rabbit. They're drinkin an smokin an sniffin glue.

Ever seen the film where the aul wimmin kill everybody an stick them all over the house? Gary Grant? *Arsenic an Lace Curtains* it's called. Anyway – see the wee guy that's Gary Grant's mental brother's pal? He's what Septic's like. Him an Mackenzie. Sactly like that. Aye that's it. *Arsenic an Lace Curtains*. Gary Grant.

Mackenzie lifts his hands out the water an he's got this big commando knife an all the water's runnin off it like Skallyburr in the King Arthur film. It's horrible. I get right scared. I don't know about Gal cos his soldiers stopped talkin at that bit.

Know what I've noticed? See when ye're terryfied? Ye remember things a lot better than when ye're not terryfied. I mean – I must've been in Glasgow a million times wi ma maw for ma birthday presents. Twenty-pound Provvy. An I can only ever remember wee bits like the movey stairs in Lewis's. But see this time wi Mackenzie – I can remember all these stupit lookin details. Mad so it is. Mad.

Mackenzie's comin at us like he's been to knife twirlin lessons. His eyes're shiny as glass ornaments. An he's got this catalogue stickin out his pocket. Mibbi he's goin to order all his Christmas present early, I thinks. Or mibbi buy a tent an fishin rods? I don't know? But I mind thinkin that's funny Mackenzie wi a catalogue. I mean yer maw an yer sisters aye! They look through catalogues for ages like witches in a spell book. But not boys. An specially not Mackenzie.

His gang get out his road an he's clumpin his boots deliberate. Gal's soldiers start talkin again. Mackenzie shoves Septic on his arse an rips a leg off the rabbit an starts bitin into it. He grins at me an I screw ma face up. The bloods dribblin down his chin.

Gal's soldiers're laughin or cryin – I can't tell. But knowin the bold Gal he's laughin. Right in Mackenzie's face. *Ha ha, Mackenzie, I hope ye choke on the fur,* I'm waitin on Gal sayin. But it's quiet an his soldiers're goin up an down.

The gang's all got Export an Pale Ale an half bottles of Buckie an they're passin them round watchin for what Mackenzie's goin to do.

This guy wi red hair starts puttin ash out the fire on his face. Indian. HOW! He's blowin this crisp poke in an out. Cheese an onion. But his eyes're starin mad. Worse than Hammer House of Horror eyes. The first I seen it – sniffin glue. I always thought ye done it wi yer nose. But this guy's suckin glue really cos the bag flattens an then he blows the air out an the bag goes up again like a balloon. Every time he takes a couple of sucks he gets slower. Now he's draggin the ash down his face that slow I can't tell if he's wantin to streak his face or stretch his skin. I can see in underneath his eyeball. It's like a wee red smile.

Gal elbows me an at the same time Mackenzie's head goes up sharp. If he had dog ears they'd've stuck up the way an alsation does it when ye whistle so its owner can't hear. It's a train. Another train.

Septic's glarin at us an keepin an eye on the fire. *Skwinty bastard*, says Gal.

What you say? goes Septic, but Mackenzie's hand comes up an shuts everybody up. It shuts us all up cos he's holdin the knife dead tight. An he's not holdin the handle – he's holdin the blade an skweezin.

Next thing he swings his arm round. Like a machine. He keeps it straight an swings it on top of the fire. Blood's runnin down an drippin off the tip of the blade. Big blots're hissin in the fire. The whole gang's scared now. Me too. Gal's the same.

I'm thinkin he's goin to chib us an he starts wipin blood on his face. The glue sucker's lookin at him like he's never met him before. Like it's just them two on the surface of the moon. Mackenzie hands the blade to Septic. Septic looks scareder than us now. He thinks he's got to chib us. Gal's pokin his elbow a lot of times in ma ribs – that's the get ready to run signal.

Blood Brothers Septic, Mackenzie goes.

Septic looks like he can't understand. But that's daft cos the whole gang knew what Mackenzie meant. Even me an Gal.

Septic takes the knife like he's an alter boy wi somethin dead holy. The *Take this all of you and drink from it – this is my blood which will be given up for you an for all* goblet. But it's Septic's blood Mackenzie wants.

The gang breathes in. Things go slow. It's like they've been breathin in for ages an widenin their eyes. Septic closes his hand round the blade an Mackenzie grins. But he's not holdin tight the way Mackenzie done he's holdin just so as it won't fall.

So Mackenzie dunts his back,

C'mon Septic – Blood Brothers!

Septic wants to cry. I know cos his eyes look the sact same as mine when I want to cry but I can't. All the cryin runs down the inside of yer face an loads up yer bottom lip. Then yer bottom lip starts tremblin wi the weight. Ma da calls it the bottom drawer bein out.

Quick Alice this laddie's got the bottom drawer out, give him a piece on jam, he'd go an that made ye worse. Ye never wanted to cry. Ye wanted to hit somebody. I wanted to rip the whole loaf. It's weird. It's not like where Alf Tupper or Wilson of the Moor do somethin an no matter who tries to make them cry or angry they just go ahead an save the world. Or a wee dog trapped on the moor. Or mibbi it's just winnin a race wi a fish supper in his hand that Alf wants to do. I try to be like comics but it's too hard. Ye could make a comic out me an Gal – the things that happens to us. A film even.

Anyway Septic's got the bottom drawer out but there's no way he's goin to cry in front of us.

Hey Mackenzie, I goes, *there Septic's got the bottom drawer out fancy shovin a big outsider on jam in his gub – shut him up? Or why not smack the lips right on him. Give him a big kiss Mackenzie.*

So an I did! I sayed nothin. I was nearly as scared as Septic. Nobody was lookin at me an Gal now. They're all lookin at Septic holdin the knife like it's a hamster he doesn't want to crush.

An another thing. Gal's told me wi his soldiers that he's nearly got the rope off. It's all happenin at once.

Mackenzie covers Septic's hands wi his hands an starts skweezin. Septic pulls back an nods like he's sayin, *Right right Mackenzie I'll do it – I don't need any help.*

Blood Brothers Mackenzie, he says. An he says it that tough I forget about him greetin. That's till I see this tear racin down his face.

He wrinkles his whole face shut an presses the knife. All the time the noise of this other train's gettin louder. Mackenzie's scannin the gang makin sure they're watchin the blood. They're kiddin on they're not scared. Like slashin a big cut in yer hand's what they do before they go to bed every night.

Here son an maw an all the sisters – take this big commando knife an slash yer hands before ye go to bed – an mind an click that telly off on yer way up – night wanes, says yer da! Aye – Popeye!

Mackenzie's eyes light up at these driplets of blood comin out. Septic's skweezin his face harder. His face makes it look like he's squeezin the knife a lot harder than he really is. Gal nudges – the ropes're off. Septic starts swayin about – like the weebles that wobble an don't fall down. Granty catches him an the knife falls in the fire. There's some blood on it. I don't think it's much but Mackenzie seems happy enough.

Mackenzie shakes hands wi Septic. He's pure white – like Dracula – an Mackenzie rubs the blood on his face an whips round *Right Lugs!* He goes, an grabs Gal. I get some fright.

The guy that's sniffin glue staggers backwards an falls in the Burn. He doesn't know where he is. He's liftin the water up an lookin at it like it's Lemon Curd or somethin.

Mackenzie's got Gal an he reaches in the fire for the knife. Gal looks like a cow in the slaughterhouse. His eyes're big an bulgy. White. That's all they are – big white pool balls stickin out his face.

Saved by the Bricklayer! Can ye believe it. Whoda thought it? Not me. Not Gal. Not nobody. Never in our puffs did we ever think we'd get saved one day by the Bricklayer. But there's Mackenzie's about to do somethin horrible.

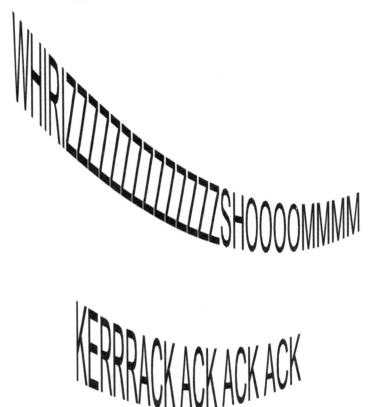

This brick hits a trunk near us. Mackenzie's got his hand near the knife. He's goin to lift it when

Whooooooooooooshkerackwhoooooooooosh

This other brick just misses me an Gal an explodes the fire everywhere.

!*!Whoosh!*! up it goes.

Wow. Mackenzie's up watchin his gang bounce away like bunnies. They're beatin red hot ashes an bits of burnin twigs off bangin into each other. All over the place they are.

Mackenzie's that mixed up he lets go of Gal an we dive in trees. But we don't run. We don't run cos of the Bricklayer. He'd take pot shots at a movin target. Ye could walk over the top of us an ye'd not know sept the ground'd be softer an mibbi a wee oof'd come out. But apart from that we were invisible.

Never attack a position uphill, ma da says.

Mackenzie's too busy tryin to stop his gang runnin in the Burn. The gluesniffer takes this deep breath an sinks under the water. The rest of them stop on the edge of the Burn cos Mackenzie's screamin an shoutin.

He's not shoutin for long cos the Bricklayer launches another volley of rocks. Like he can suddenly see Mackenzie through a gap. The mountain peaks must've blocked his view. But not now. Christ it's like a shower of meteorites now.

First Mackenzie shouts,

BRIIIIIIIIIIIIIIIIIIIIIIIIIIIIIIIIIIIIIIIIIIIIIIIIICK!

Me an the Gal's wrigglin backwards under the leaves. Bellyflappin. It's just our heads that's up. The gang're screamin in a shower of tree-bark sharpnel. Like big wanes. They all scream an jump in the Burn. Mackenzie must be fit cos he's last in an first out.

The train's away an Mackenzie's crawlin about in the dusty slag makin commando signs. He's all white. Me an Gal stay dead still cos he's scannin for us. I can see the evil beamin out his glassy eyes. An he's got the knife. It glints a couple of times like it's got a brain. Like it wants to tell me an Gal we're dead men. Mackenzie hated us. Specially since we got Mad Wilma to cave his ribs in wi his slug gun. Fenians he used to call us. Or wee Papes. Or Tague bastards. An now we've seen him gettin tanked wi the Bricklayer there's no walkin the streets for us. Unless they stick him back inside. Nut case.

They move off wi Mackenzie leadin the way an swipin his knife at bushes that won't get out the road. A big clump of red rosiedendron flowers thumps onto the grass.

Handfuls of dust

We come out of hidin. Gal looks at me wi his head tilted
down an to the side a bit an he's blowin air out his mouth.
His mouth looks like a fish. He's brushin leafs off an he
knows we're dead far as Mackenzie's concerned. Dead men.
Gal looks about. He does his big scan. He does his big scan
cos we've never been in the Slaggy before. Sept for the Pipe
an that doesn't count. He stretches his neck right out the way
a swan's is an he turns his head slow from left to right an
then from right to left. An he makes his eyes wee slits like
Chinkees or Japs. *Chinees Japaneese dirty knees look at these,* I
usually say, but he's not in the mood. I don't know why he
makes his eyes wee. Mibbi it's so's no flies can fly in an
waste his concentration – or midges. I hate midges.

All clear, says Gal, in his James Bond voice. I'm just about
to go on about how it was a close shave an we nearly got kilt
an how good he was untyin the ropes like Tonto. But I'd
need to say he was The Lone Ranger cos he never liked being
Tonto. I could be Tonto no bother. It never bothered me bein
Tonto. I mean ye couldn't get a better The Lone Ranger than
Gal. No sir. He's the best. But I'm just about to boost him up
an he bends down an picks up the poke of glue. Cheese an
onion. I don't say nothin. I know it's not right. I mean
anybody that had a maw in Coatbrig knew sniffin the glue's
not right.

If I ever catch ye at that glue sniffin I'll kill ye, ma maw goes.

An that was what it was like for Gal an all. His brothers all liked the Buckie but they never sniffed glue. They battered glue sniffers for fun. Kicked Doods off the Pipe this night. Without even a warnin.

Doods is sittin wi his feet danglin where it goes over for the third time. He's got a Ready Salted at his gub sniffin away. Jim Gal goes by.

Right Doods?

Riiight Gaaaall.

BOOT.

Quiet bit.

SPELASHSH

An there's Doods wrigglin on the rocks wi water runnin in his mouth. Nearly choked the doctor says after he put on the stookies. *The only thing holdin him thegether was the glue,* Jim Gal says.

So that's all goin through ma head when Gal's sniffin away at the bag. His eyes go different. I'm thinkin about how to say I don't want none. But he doesn't ask me he lobs it in the air an boots it in the Burn. *Ta ta glue poke, see if ye can find wee Doods in there,* he goes an laughs a strange laugh wi his face to the sky.

I don't mention it. Me an Gal were good at that – not mentionin things that ye knew the other one never wanted mentioned. This was one of them times. There's this glue tin an he pours what's left in the fire. It goes up wi a trail of black smoke. An that's when I thought **Evil Stick** Black smoke. It's from Hell. The smoke's a black snake wrigglin out the ground an the Slaggy's ashes out of Hell an the Devil's just below the crusty surface makin pots of bubblin Evil Stick in wee red tins an givin them to Mackenzie's gang.

Whoa – there I go again. I'm always thinkin mad things. They'll be lockin me up so they will. Heartwood. Throw the key away probably.

I'm just gettin over the glue when what does he do? Only bends down an lifts a half bottle of Buckie. It's been slung. He takes a swig an stuffs it down his trousers. Anybody that seen the roastin Big Gal got off Maw Gal for drinkin'd think Gal was mad for doin it.

An all he can do after the swig is give me a what're you lookin at look an say *C'mon,* an head off. An where does he head off? Not back up the railway an the Oil Pond. No. Right in the Slaggy. Right the very way Mackenzie went. I'm tellin ye! I'm startin to wonder about him so I am. Really startin to wonder.

I feel like sayin to Gal I'm goin back on ma own. All this sniffin glue an drinkin Buckie's not right so it's not. But we never go unless it's the two of us. Ma head's doin somersaults. It starts goin haywire again.

Remember the rabbit? Remember Mackenzie rippin a leg off of it? Well I hears another leg gettin ripped off. This shiver rubs the hairs on ma neck the wrong way up. I'm hot but I'm cold. Gal's twenty feet away movin deeper into the Slaggy. I feels breath on the back of ma neck. I'm rooted. I hears movin about at the fire. It's the Devil. Aul Nick. Must be.

I turns.

Fire's the same. Rabbit's the same. See ma magination! The only thing's this big dry toad crickin away doin toad poems. That's what ma da calls them – toad poems. *Ribbit ribbit ribbit dibbit-ity croakity doo,* he goes.

So after ma magination tricks me I turn an run after Gal. Even if I do know it's nothin I'm still scared. I feel like there's somethin goin to happen. Don't ask me why.

We're dossin through the trees an Gal's not sayin nothin. Sometimes he never sayed nothin for ages then he sayed hunners of things. But this time he's not sayin nothin so I goes, *Gal d'you believe in planets?*

He looks at me wi half his lips turned up.

Planets – d'ye believe in them – spacemen an that?

He wonders. He's thinkin if he believes in them or not. It's not like what team d'ye support when ye can just go Celtic. This is a question that he needs to think about.

Planets?

Aye.

Spacemen?

Aye!

He looks up like the answer's wrote in the sky. Well it probably is – in alien cloud language we can't read.

HERE WE ARE YA DAFT BASTARDS

Like me an Gal in the pet shop. Talking to the fish. They know ye're talkin but they can't understand a word.

BLOOP BLOOP, is what they say back.

Hello wee fishes, we go, *fancy comin down to ma house to stay?*

They wee neons – magic so they are. I like talkin to them. We're gettin a fish tank when ma da gets better ma maw says. We're puttin it in the kitchen when he moves his bed back up to his room.

Hello wee light bulbs. It's a wonder they don't electroshoot theirselfs all electric an under the water like that. Gal says ye could hang them off the Christmas tree. That's mad – all them wee Christmas lights quiverin about.

There's these other fish that eat all the slime off the sides.

God you're the ugliest fish I ever seen in ma natch – Gal c'mere an see this!

Hello wee facelift fishy. You look like Septic.

That's how they're Septicfish now. We slagged it rotten
but it just looked at us. Called it all the names under the sun
but it'd just blink away like we were sayin,
*My My you're the prettiest fish in the whole Pet Shop. Aren't
you?*
Gal's still thinkin if he believes in planets an spacemen. I
decides to hurry him up.
Saturn Jupiter Mars Venus Earth.
I know thaaaat!
Mercury Pluto Neptune.
I knowwwwwwwwwww!
Oops! I decided not to hurry him up. So we're walkin
along an I'm lookin up at the Lofty Peaks. It's like
Switzerland or the Everests or somethin. All these pointy
hills, pure white like macaroon. An a burn runnin through
the middle an all these trees an ruins. Gal says they're old
ironworks but they look like the Roman Forts we got at
school.
Our Jim says they're ironworks.
He flings a stone.
Roman forts.
Ironworks.
He flings a stone.
Roman forts.
Ironworks.
He flings a stone.
Roman forts.
Ironworks, he flings a stone, *Roman forts.*
Ironworks, he flings a stone, *Roman forts.*
Ironworks, he flings a stone, *RomanfortsIronworks,* he flings
a stone, *Roman forts.*

Ironworks.
Now he's flingin handfuls of dust in the Burn cos he's
pickin up the stones too fast.
I got feart in case Mackenzie heard us. I let him win. When
ye let Gal win he always swaggered away grinnin. But that

would be only for a wee while an he'd be all right. Like he never wanted to be the winner really. Like he wanted to loss all along. He'd be dead nice after he won. Treat me like I won. Mad. Can't understand it all half the time so I can't.

We stops at this wall that goes along the Burn. There's a wee lip at the bottom. Only enough room for one shoe an then it's the Burn. So me an Gal's goin along wi our arms flat on the wall like Spiderman. Facin it. We're scrapin our cheeks along to keep the balance. Funny I never knew a wall had a smell. It smells like salty rock. He's first an I'm after him. Fingertips touchin. He's lookin but all I can see is the wall wi one eye an the Burn wi the other eye an Gal's head bobbin forward wi every step. Septic'd be good at this.

Gal comes to the Echo. Me an Gal used to tell everybody we'd been up it. Everybody sayed they were up it. If everybody that says they were up it wasn't tellin lies it'd be the most visited place in Scotland. Gal pulls me up to the ledge. This time it's empty.

We peers in. Ye can hear the clickin toenails of rats zoomin through the dark O. Gal's peerin eyes probably look like a cartoon to them. On a round telly.

He makes a hand funnel. *Ga-al ruu-ules.*

Nothin. Just the tippity-tap of feet disappearin an drips of water. Ye can hear the rats sittin up an listenin – brushin the slime wi their wormy tails an makin rat plans.

He looks at me.

I shrugs.

Mibbi it's not workin Ga...

Gal Gal Gal Gal Rules Rules *Rules Rules*, the Echo goes.

Me an him's got big open faces. The words come out an fall in the Burn. Splashin. Swear! I saw ripples.

I has a go.

Ga-al's Men-tal.

There's this big silent an the drip drip of water. Ye can't tell real drips from the echo of other drips or the echo of the echo of drips or what. Then,

Ga-al's Ga-al's Men-tal Men-tal

Waw-eee, says Gal an we whistle up it, spit, fart, chuck rocks an sing...

𝄞 *When I was a biddy widdy boy*
Ma grandmother bought me a cute little toy
silver bells hangin on a string
she told me it was ma ding a ling a ling.
The top our lungs's burstin.
Nothin.
It comes back out all mixed up.

𝄞 *When I was   a biddy widdy boy*
Ma
When I   was a biddy widdy
boy
Ma
When I was a   biddy   widdy boy
Ma   grandmother bought me a cute
little toy
silver
When I   was a biddy widdy boy
Ma   grandmother bought me a cute
little toy
silver   bells hangin
on a string
she told   me it   was ma ding a ling a ling
When I was a biddy widdy boy   widdy boy
Ma me a   cute

little toy
silver bells hangin on a string
she told me it was ma   *ding a ling a ling* *was ma*
ding a ling a ling   *bells hangin on a string*
When I

When I was a   *biddy widdy boy*
Ma   *grandmother bought me a cute little toy*
silver bells hangin on a string
she told me it was ma *ding a ling a ling* *boy*
When I was a biddy   *widdy boy*
Ma grandmother bought me a cute little toy
silver bells hangin on a string
she told ding a   *ling a ling*
When I was a biddy widdy boy   *she told a string*
she told me it was ma   *ding a ling a ling.*

Wow! Wild. We farted up a some more times. An after Gal clanged an aul fryin pan we couldn't think of anythin else. So we're lyin lookin through green slime at sticklebacks glidin over the tops of ASDA trolleys an rusty aul bin lids.

Aye, says Gal out the blue.

Eh?

Aye – Planets an that, I do believe in them.

I liked that answer. I hated when Gal never believed in somethin. I wanted him to believe in all what I believed in. An me to believe in all the things he believed in. I wanted us the sact same so I did. Sact same.

That's mad Gal ma man we're the sact same again.

An we shook hands an done Alf Tupper an Billy Whizz.

We're always the sact same that right Gal?

Aye everythin – same at fightin.

We always took a draw at fightin. Every time without fail.

Christ Gal we even fart the same.

Gal thought that was the funniest thing ever.

Brbrbrbrbrbrrb he says wi his mouth up the tunnel.

Brbrbrbrbrbrrb, I says back.

We fall about laughin.

Brbrbrbrbrbrrb.

Brbrbrbrbrbrrb.

We fall about laughin.

Brbrbrbrbrbrrb.

Brbrbrbrbrbrrb.

We fall about laughin.

An that's us for ages kiddin on we're fartin up this tunnel an fallin about laughin. We never bothered about nothin. Not even Mackenzie. After ages I asks Gal a question that stumps him. About birds fartin.

Gal? See birds? Do they fart?

Eh eh eh, he just goes an that's him. We sat for ages an ages but none of us could remember a bird fartin.

Itchycooblue

We've stopped at this Roman Ruin Gal says is an ironworks but we can't be bothered arguin cos the Echo Tunnel's the happiest we've been for ages. We don't want to waste it.

But we don't say nothin about it to each other. Can ye magine it?

Oh by the way Gal that's the happiest I've been for years old bean – in fact I think it's the happiest we've been as pals for ages what d'ye think?

Here's what I think – thud *–* a swift kick on the balls.

He's lyin back on the stones an I'm starin at the Peak. Twice the size of all the rest. One end's just this straight cliff. The sun's shinin round the edges. It's this thick line of red. Like wanes do wi magic markers when they're drawin.

Gal's sunbathin on the stones. I lies down an puts ma hands behind ma head. There's thick moss on this bit of the wall an ma fingers sink right in. The bony bits of ma knuckles're shapin into cold cushiony stuff. I'm a yunk in a nest waitin for ma da to come back wi some worms. Or crunchy flies. Yum yum.

Zzzzzzzzzzzzzzzzzz
zzzzzzzzzzzzzzzzzzz
zzzzzzzzzzzzzzzzzzz
zzzzz

The Peak starts crumblin an falls down at us. It's gettin darker an darker. I'm tryin to scream to Gal to get up an run but I'm paralysed. I wakes up wi this big scud an then another one an there's Gal flingin sods at me.

Diiiiiiirt Bomb, he's goin hurlin more.

I starts pickin up bits of dirt an flingin them back but they're powderin an it's just these clouds I'm flingin. Anyway, he's offski in the trees an shoutin *Dreeemer dreeemer*. Afore ye can say th- th- th- that's all folks the trees've stopped movin. Just for that wee minute I feel all alone. Spooky. Like it's me on this other planet an nobody nowhere. There's a burn but there's nothin in it an no birds or rabbits or frogs or newts. Not even Mackenzie. I look all about an there's nothin livin on the whole place. The Burn's like the water ye boil the tatties in. Nothin in it. Just dirt. The sky's got no birds an the bushes're still. They're plastic the bushes. That's what they are. Plastic.

Next thing Gal appears on the start of the slope up the Peak. I can see his red sloppy joe. It's like the sloppy joe's alive an it's climbin.

Oh I know, says the red sloppy Joe – *now that I'm alive I'll climb this big white mountain an stick out like a sore thumb.* Then

71

I looks up an it's a blot of blood creepin up a giant raggity skull. It shakes ma head like a horse.

Gal thinks he's hidin so I dive in the trees an go through the branches runnin an pullin at the same time. Anybody'd wonder how I could move that fast through trees.

Gal's covered wi jaggy nettles when I springs out. He's bent over stretchin his top lip along his teeth. Except the ones that weren't there. Ma maw says it's the IRN BRU that does that. But she's mental. Everybody knows IRN BRU's good for ye. They've got a runner on the label – white vest an shorts.

Gal's rubbin this dokey leaf down his leg. He looks over like he wants me to help. What can I do? Once the blotches're there that's it. Ye can only rub the leaf for ages an hope it goes away. I rip out dokeys anyway so I look like I'm helpin. It's not like I wanted to not help him. But sometimes when mibbi somebody falls an splits their head ye don't know what to do. Ye want to run an get somethin but ye're froze. An big people're away gettin all the stuff. Well, see when that happens to me, I can't stop laughin sometimes. I know it's not right cos mibbi there's gallons of blood all over the pavement an runnin in the snow. An mibbi it's an aul wummin or somethin but I can't stop laughin. *Don't you laugh,* I say to maself but it's no use. *Hee hee hee,* I start goin an cos I'm froze everybody sees me. But they kid on they don't. Christ! Magine me in the Jack an Jill story? Jack an Jill went up the hill to fetch a pail of water. Jack fell down an broke his crown an Derrick stood there like a laughin-faced hyena!

Or Humpty Dumpty sat on the wall an had this fall an Derrick Daniel Riley stood there laughin till he cried. Slappin his thighs. All the kings horses an all the kings men sayed they were goin to tell his maw.

Or Little Bo Peep greetin an me laughin ma head off – rollin up an down the wee hills. An her skippin about lookin for her sheep. I'd be laughin that much they'd need to carry me to some other nursery rhyme that's all happy. That would wipe the smile off ma face. Probably.

An another thing – what about these sheep that come home if ye leave them alone? They're always waggin their tails behind them – well it'd be a bit mad if they were waggin their tails in front of them.

But Gal's in agony an I'm pickin dokeys.

You're laughin, he goes.

I'm pickin dokeys!

But ye're laughin at me.

I'm pickin dokeys, I says keepin ma back to him.

I can see yer soldiers.

So that's that.

Haaaaaaaaaaaaaaaaaaaaaaaaaaaaaaaaaaaaaaaaaaaaaa aaaaaaaaaaaaaaaaaaaaaaaaaaaaaaaaaaaa,

I goes an turns round tryin to straighten up.

What is it? Eh? D'ye think it's funny? It's not that when you fall in the jaggies is it!!

He starts doin me.

Oh Oh Gal Gal I've fell in the jaggies Oh Oh help me please.

But the tears're streamin down ma face. That's when he sings this song that he heard ma maw singin one day. It gets right on ma wick.

Send for the amblence driiiiiiiiiiiiiiiiiiiiiiiiiiiiiiiiii ver
send for the amblence driiiiiiiiiiiiiiiiiiiiiiiiiiiiiiiiii ver
our wee Derrick's skint his knee
send for the amblence driiiiiiiiiiiiiiiiiiiiiiiiiiiiiiiiii ver.

Even if it's annoyin me I can't stop laughin. Cos Gal can't sing it right for the blotches. I don't know how I think things like that're funny. That's the way it is in ma head. I've got one mental head me so I have. One mental head.

Gal marches over an picks up all the dokeys that's lyin where I've been rollin. Petted lip – bottom drawer – mind that? Well he's got this one THAT size. He gets all the dokeys an rips them up an flings them in the trees. **Well!!** I go in hisderricks.

He jumps on me an pins ma arms to the ground wi his knees.

Who's the king? he goes.

Haaaaaaaaaaaaaaaaaaaaaaaaaaaaaaaaaaaaaaaaaaaaaaaaaaaaaaaaaaa.

Who is it? he says twistin ma ear an pressin ma nose in.

Haaaaaaaaaaaaaaaaaaaaaaaaaaaaaaaaaaaaaaaaaaaaaaaaaaaaaaaaaaa.

He starts rippin out lumps of grass an stuffin them in ma gub. Know how when ye're laughin ye can't flick a fly off a table? Well that's me. Weak as a mitten. He's stuffin enough grass in ma mouth to choke a horse but ma laugh's snufflin through it.

Hammmamamammmmmmmaaaaaammmmmm, I'm goin.

I starts chokin – half real half on purpose. But it's not workin' he's rippin bigger bits an stuffin them in.

Ye're not laughin now Riley?

He asks some mad questions. That's mad for two reasons:

1   He can see I'm not laughin now cos I'm chokin.

2   Cos I'm chokin I can't answer anyhow.

I tries stoppin breathin an bulgin eyes. He laughs an stuffs more grass. For a minute I thinks he's goin to kill me. But I can stop breathin better than anybody. An I can poke ma eyes out on brush poles. He stops stuffin grass in an jumps up. I keep ma eyes bulged as anythin an keep on not breathin. He thinks he's kilt me. Man ye should've seen his face when I spray the grass out like a green fountain an sook ma eyes back in. He starts laughin. An while he's laughin he looks down at his leg an the blotches're away. He looks at me like it's magic an bursts out laughin again. I don't dive at him now. That's what ye're supposed to do. But we're different me an Gal.

We get to the Burn an we sit down again. I'm throwin wee helicopters up an watchin them birl down in the Burn. They land an send out sonar ripples an float away. It doesn't sound much but it's great. Ma da showed me.

Here Gal – helicopters! I go but he's not botherin. Sometimes he's like that. Stares away in the distance. I used to think he was watchin mibbi a bird or a rabbit or a nest that's too far away for anybody else. But that's not it. He just stares like he's peerin at a wee pair of yella eyes glarin back at him out the black bars between the trees. An there's no talkin to him. He grunts or sometimes swears. Swearin a lot more now Gal. He's a trooper.

You stay away from him, ma granny says, *he swears like a buckin trooper. I don't like laddies that swear.* Ma granny always says Buckin instead of that other word.

Fuckin.

That word.

Gal says it all the time. An Bastard pish fart an shite.

But they're not like.

Fuckin.

Ma da'd kill me if he heard me at it.

See that day. Lyin at the bottom of the Peak wi Gal – even if he wasn't talkin. It was the best. All this sun's on the ground like leopard spots. Except they're black an the sun's gold – but that's what they were like – all over the place. If ye half shut yer eyes it looked like an ocean surface. An if ye half shut yer ears the Burn was waves an the Peak was a big island pokin out a misty sea.

Half shut yer eyes Gal.

Nothin.

Gal half shut yer eyes the grass looks like the sea.

He grunts an keeps starin.

See if ye half shut yer eyes an ears...

Fuck up! he goes. So I ignore him. Anyway if he wanted to half shut his ears he'd need to have a Closin Day. Wing nut. But even if I was in the huff cos he swore at me it was still the best day. No Mackenzie. White clouds bumpin into each other makin pictures an headin off as other pictures.

After. I tried stickin a buttercup under Gal's chin see if he liked butter. But all that ended up was this buttercup flattenin under his chin an him pointin his chin up a wee bit in the huff.

I decides to go into ma own wee dream world.

Go in yer own wee dream world, I says to ma head. I picks this dandelion fluff clock an starts blowin it. All the wee white bits start floatin away. They're miniature microscopic parashooters. There's this big white parashoot an a wee man hangin there. It's a seed really but ye don't need a good magination to see it's a parashooter an all his pals. An they're all worried cos they're not goin down like they should be. To take on the Gerries – ah ah ah ah – wi their Tommy guns firin an landin in haystacks. An big barns wi pigeons flappin out. An down some wummin's chimney. When she's makin bread. But they're not goin down – they're goin sideways. That's how they're worried.

Probably land in the wrong country. Mibbi on some miniature wummin comin out the miniature chip-shop wi a tiny poke of chips an a wee dog an they're lookin up wonderin what the hell this is all about, all these parashooters shootin up the pavement.

But that's not what I'm doin. I'm blowin to see what time it is. If ye don't want it to be parashooters ye can use it as a clock. How many times ye take to blow the things off is what time it is.

Whaaaw.
Whaaaw.
Whaaaw.
It's three o' clock Gal.

He looks at me. I poke the thing in the air.

He looks at the empty fluff clock an all the parashooters floatin over the Burn. Shakes his head. But here's the thing. He doesn't shake his head like the way ye always do if ye're a laddie. He shakes it like he's ma da an I'm caught tryin to use his good saw to cut through a drainer lid.

I gives him the what're you lookin at me as if ye're ma da catchin me sawin a drainer lid for. Ye do that like this – see the way Elvis turns up his lip? Right – well ye turn both ends of yer lip up like that. Then ye let yer chin drop till it's nearly hittin off yer chest. But it's the last thing that makes it a good question mark look. Ye pull yer eyebrows thegether an make yer eyes look at each other.

Gal's not carin. *D'you still believe in that stuff?* he goes, an nods at the bewildered parashooters.

Sometimes I don't bother about nothin nobody says. But this time I feels throat lumps. But not the throat lumps ye get watchin *Bambi*. It's a lump that wants to scud Gal wi a chunk of the slag that's lyin about like moonrock. An when I'm doin it I'll be goin

One o' clock,
smash wi the rock.

Two o' clock,
smash wi the rock.

Three o' clock,
smash wi the rock.

Time for bed Gallacher!
Last big smash wi the rock.

But I don't want him to know I'm like that. I used to be able to tell Gal everythin. Well nearly everythin. Not the likes of greetin at *Bambi*. Magine it:

Oh by the way Gal old bean I had a right good greet at Bambi *there hand me the handkerchiefs would you?*

Right into school he'd go,

He was greetin at Bambi.

Ha ha ha ha ha ha, goes everybody in the dinner queue.

So I smile like the Joker an pick another one an start blowin it. Gal gives it the sact same shake of the head.

Is that the only head shake you know ya tube? I says.

Well I never really. I only sayed it into maself cos I was still doin the Joker smile. This time it's five o' clock. They're not that good for tellin the time the fluff clocks.

After. We're goin through the Slaggy for ages. Sometimes there's big high walls that Gal says're old cottages but they look like Aztec ruins to me. Covered in trees an ivy an moss. They look like they punched theirselfs up out the slag at a mad angle.

We're walkin along this wall. It's wee so I jump off it before him an

kerrunchchcshshsz

I'm in this pile of stuff. The stuff they put on roofs. The stuff ma da worked wi for years. Gal's lookin down laughin at me. I'm up to ma knees in it. It's like I've fell through the ice up the Lochs. But this ice is dry an warm cos the sun's been shinin on it.

Geronimo! Gal shouts an he **kerunshes** in too.

I tells him this story. An it's mad. We don't move. The

stuff's jaggin right in but none of us says *it's sore* or makes a
that's sore face. An at the end we're still up to our knees in it.
The story's all about ma da. He was workin on the side.
He left the house when it was dark an sneaked up the
Boltwork. A different way every day he went. Anyway, he's
on the Boltwork roof puttin sheets of the stuff we're standin
in on broke bits. The Boltwork was made out of red bricks.
Zillions. Ye could see it from ma granny's back across the
railway. It was like a giant saw. It was like it was sawin the
sky. The Boltwork roof was a lot of roofs really. All shaped
like the teeth of a saw.

We were all wavin out ma granny's back. He waved back.
That was the same day his pal got kilt.

They got an end of a sheet each an started walkin down
the slope wi it. But there's this scream that goes on for ages
ma da says takin a slug of whisky out the bottle ma granda's
got. Then the sheet falls at the other end an breaks. *Sactly a
third along the sheet Danny,* ma da keeps sayin to ma granda;
sactly a third along the sheet. An ma granda's noddin. An ma
da looks an there's no pal. Just this hole in the roof that the
sheet was coverin. His pal fell through the hole an landed on
all the machines. Dead. An ma da was greetin. An there's
another funny thing. I mean – if I greet all ma pals slag me.
So here's ma da an all these big people an he's greetin – I
mean who's ever seen their da greetin? Right nobody. But
nobody notices that he's greetin sept me. So I goes in the bog
– I was only wee – an I gets this bit of bog paper. An this is
the maddest bit – when I give him the bog paper he laughs
an everybody laughs an it's like they're all havin the best
time ever talkin about ma da's pal that fell through the roof.
Sometimes I can't make out big people at all.

After I tell the story Gal's got his mouth wide open.
Amazin.

Yer da was cryin?

Aye.

Yer da was cryin?

Aye.

Out loud?

A bit.

He puts his hands on his hips an stares at the sky an I put ma hands on mine an look the other way. I look the other way for ages but then ma leg starts itchin like mad. Gal's too. We starts scratchin like lousy dogs. We crunch out the stuff an there's millions of it all over the place.

Gal bends down an breaks a bit off. He inspects it. He's great at inspectin Gal. He inspects things for hours sometimes without sayin anythin. He turns it round an round like a scientist.

Then his eyes light up. If he was a cartoon or a comic this bulb'd light up above his head. Well it wouldn't light up it'd just have these straight lines comin out like a star an that would make ye think it was lut up. I mean c'mon – magine a bulb lightin up in a comic? Ye'd throw it on the floor an run out yer room screamin. Cartoons're different. They can do it easy.

So Gal's got this bright idea an I've got wide eyes waitin for it. He holds the grey-blue stuff up at ma nose. Nearly right up ma nose in fact.

Itchycooblue man! Wrecks yer lungs an kills ye, he goes. *Don't breathe it in.*

The two of us suck in air an crunch away. We're well away before breathin. We held our breaths that long that we needed hundreds of it when we started breathin again. Man we're suckin that much in all the birds start faintin an fallin out the trees.

Choppers

The Burn's a oasis. A paintin. That's before ye get the sun out yer eyes. Then it's foam, bricks, slime, prams, bikes an washin machines. This chopper's stickin its handlebars through the frogspawn like a mad animal. Steel antlers an stuff hangin down like gigantic green slabbers.

This Donny Osmond LP floats by. All the lassies loved him. The Osmonds. The street empties of lassies every time it comes on. But they're not on any more. It's the Jackson Five now.

Die Donny!!! we shouts an rocks it till it sinks –

baluirp! Below the jelly surface. But even if it is black boggin, some bits ye can still see yer face in it. Like a black funeral car – ye can see yer face in it nearly as good as a mirror.

We're lookin at each others faces.

You look mad, goes Gal. But he looked madder than me. He always looked madder than me.

You look madder than me Gal, I goes. So he messes the flatness of the water so our faces go like crumpled washin.

It's good cos the water starts to get quiet again an yer face starts to not be crumpled washin any more. One minute it's all these lines wavin like pet shop fish an next thing there's yer face. Like the beginnin of Dr Who when it goes:

WHOO HOO WHOO HOO WHOO HOO HOO HOO HOO HOO

an his face makes itself up on the screen. Or *Bonanza* backwards.

Me an Gal's amazin. So when our faces're back it's this amazin face lookin at this other amazin face.

♪ *A-A-maze-in-in, face,* Gal starts singin an pointin

at mine. I can't think of nothin to say back. He nearly always had the best patter Gal. His big brothers taught him patter. Sometimes he'd say a joke or somethin funny an all the big people'd laugh but I'd not get it. So I'd look at him like as if he mibbi would splain it to me. But he never had a scooby either. His brothers were always doin that – tellin him somethin to say that was funny but not tellin him how it was funny. I don't know.

That members me of when ma maw always sent me to Gribben's when I was wee. I used to memorise it.

Two dozen rolls three pints of milk a block of butter five senior service an a packet of doctor white super please.

Gribbin an his two sisters'd smile. I think he was a bit deaf. He'd go, *Say that again son?*

I'd take a deep breath an say it all again.

Two dozen rolls three pints of milk a block of butter five senior service an a packet of doctor white super please.

But then he'd put a hand up at his ear an say, *What was that?*

The wimmin'd be laughin when Gribben's puttin the rolls in a poke an gettin the butter. Sometimes they'd lean over an whisper in other customer's ears an they'd look over an laugh. I always went hot an couldn't wait to get out.

Gribbin'd leave the Doctor White Super till the end an wrap it up in newspaper. He'd always cough a couple of times when he done that. Every single time. I never got the Doctor White Supers all the time. It'd be just *Two dozen rolls three pints of milk a block of butter an five senior service,* for weeks an then all of a sudden it'd be, *Two dozen rolls three pints of milk a block of butter five senior service an a packet of doctor white super please.* Then just as quick there'd be no Doctor White Super for ages.

I went in the house this day an says to ma maw, *I'm not askin for doctor white super any more.*

Ma auntie Sadie's there. Ma maw looks at me.

How not son?

Cos they all laugh at me in the shop.

Sadie bursts out laughin. I can't believe it. There's molten metal comin up ma body. Laughed at in the shop an laughed at in the house. Anyway. That's the last I heard of Doctor White Super till Danny Garrett says what they were. Make ye sick.

But I was tellin ye about makin faces in the Burn. Gal's still singin amazin face. Next thing like magic his ears turn into these big handles. Silver. An his face is the European Cup an there's Billy McNeil holdin it up – but it's Gal's head. That's the first time he got called the European Cup. It was me. I done it.

You look like... like... the European Cup. Man we should've fell about the place but he just stared deep in the water lookin for a good slag to fire back at me. All he could come up wi was the melted basin joke. Even ma wee sisters knew that one. It was nothin. It was good the first time but not the zilkilionth time an not off Gal when he's usually good. That's somethin I've noticed about people. They're great at slaggin ye till ye hit them wi a stormer an then they come away wi all the aul jokes. Like ye zapped the power out them wi the snappy line. Like it's kryptonite.

He knows he's beat an stares even harder in the Burn this time. Like he's tryin to boil the water wi his eyes.

I finds this bit of mirror an starts flickin light about. Up under trees. There's this bit where a big thick branch comes out an I'm flickin the light up under its oxters.

Mind an wash under yer oxters! ma maw shouts when ye're gettin washed for mass.

I always think Oxters an Oxtail soup're the same. I'm mad me. I mean they're nothin like each other but sometimes I'm in the bog an I burst out laughin an ma maw's shoutin *What're you doin in there boy?* An I shout, *Nothin,* an the soldiers're goin up an down. It's only cos I'm maginin all this oxtail soup pourin out from under ma arms every time I lift one up to wash. The bath's full to the brim wi the stuff – like smooth die a rear.

There I'm away again. All I'm sayin is that I'm flickin this light under this tree's oxters an I'm thinkin that this is the first light that's ever been shone up there. That made me dead important in ma head. I mean nobody might never ever shine no light up there ever again. That means I'm the only person in the world to shine light up there. I starts lookin about for places to shine light where nobody else has. To boldly go where no light flicker has gone before. Up under that bit at the roots that looks like an alien's hand grabbin onto the planet. It's the bit where rabbits an things live in cartoons. It's great. There's millions of places where light's never got shone on.

I'm on ma side. Then ma other side. Then upside down – shinin this wee jaggy bit of light. An what's Gal up to? Member the wine? He's swiggin out that an starin in the Burn. An here's the thing – he's sittin the same way when ye stare hopin somebody'll say

What's the matter wi you? so ye can say,
Nothin.
Are ye sure?
Aye.

But really ye want them to ask three or four times so ye can say ye never got a biscuit or ye've no money for the pictures.

That's the way Gal looks like he's sittin. But he's not cos when he sits like that an ye ask him what's wrong he can't hear ye. He must have this switch inside his head an he switches all his outside bits off wi it. Even his eyes. When ye wave yer hand in front of his face he can't see it.

I mean if ye flattened him wi a big lump of wood he'd jump up screamin. I'm not sayin he's Kwai Chang Caine or somethin that can't feel pain. All I'm sayin is he stares in the distance.

That's it – he stares in the distance.

He's swiggin Buckie like half of him knows he's swiggin an half of him doesn't.

He didn't like me callin him the European Cup cos after a couple more swigs I'm watchin him out the wee bit of mirror. He looks to see I'm not watchin an leans over the Burn. He turns his head slow to the right. He turns it slow to the left. Then he starts flickin his ears an lookin at them movin. I was goin to shout somethin about watch ye don't start a gale force wind or Dumbo or somethin but it's a good job I never cos his face goes all angry an he flings the wine bottle through his reflection.

He watches the waves slowin down an turns at me. But this is a look I don't know. I wish there was a dictionary of looks so I could tell ye what it was. All I can say is it was a cross between a help me look an a get out ma road look an chirio look. Mad.

I gives him a shrug. That can mean anythin. I never knew what he wanted me to say. I turns away an starts flickin the light. But the light was shakin like it was on a train. That was me not greetin. I'm great at not greetin me. It's like not laughin only yer soldiers don't go up an down. There's this twin tub washin machine inside ye an it's goin like the clappers an you're a big jelly tryin to keep from vibratin. Mission Impossible.

It's ages we're like that. Then I notice his eyes're all glassy but there's a wee smile on his face. So I flick the light in his eyes just to see what he's like.

Beat it.

I'm not sure what kind of beat it he means so I shine again. He turns away. He'll be alright for a laugh in ten minutes.

I'm starin in the Burn lookin at how the reflection of the whole Slaggy plummets down like the Burn's a deep ravine. The Grand Canyon in America. Me an Gal's goin there when we're millionaires. We're goin to be cowpokes for John Wayne.

Gal look at these trees how far into the Burn they go!

He says nothin.

D'ye think the Burn's deep as that?

He moves. I'm gettin an answer. Great!

It's a reflection. The Burn's only four feet here.

I feels good now. It might be nothin to you but he's talkin an that's somethin. It really is somethin. I keeps it goin.

But how can it reflect a big tree if it's four feet?

Who cares? goes Gal. But that's good. I give it quiet for a minute till ye just know he's listenin. We're that quiet all the birds an stuff start comin back. But it's a quick retreat when I starts talkin again.

Know what I'd like to do Gal?

No. An I don't want to know either.

I lean right over the Burn. I lean that far I look like I'll fall in. He moves. He doesn't jump up to save me. He moves his arm back an out to the side they way ye do when ye're goin to get up off the ground. But he stops when he sees it's a plan.

I'd like to jump right in an fall an fall an mibbi catch one of them branches on the way by an pull a couple of leaves off it an keep fallin an fallin an land on that big white puff cloud there an sponge right into it.

That right? Gimmi a shout when ye hit the rocks wi a hell of a skelp.

I start flickin the light again cos he's comin back to hiself.

This Moorhen Flaps up The Burn.

It's a foot above the surface an right in the middle. Next thing it goes *KER-ROCK KER-ROCK*. Me an Gal's connected to the same radar. Our heads swing it into the distance an Gal's up sharp an quiet peerin through the trees. He can still see it. All I can see is the leaves rattlin against each other in the tube of breeze that its wings left.

Gal starts movin along the Burn. I'm behind him. Not like a shot cos we're paddin wi elastic legs an puttin our feet down easy. Like Bugs Bunny dead slow. The reason we're runnin like elastic men is Mackenzie an his gang.

Moorhen

The Burn's gettin deep an wide an frightenin. We're springin quiet along the bank.

The water's dark

an slow.

We stop at the corner an flop on the grass. It's more knackerin runnin quiet than runnin ordinary. I'm breathin wi a wide mouth like Big Danny Malloy eatin his breakfast. Same age as us an he gets his cornflakes in a Pyrex dish.

The Slaggy's reflected on the black water. An upside down paintin it's like. It's only this island in the middle that reminds ye it's a river. The water's got to bend round it. If ye've got a magination it's a big green grassy comet an the foamin water bendin round's the tail.

Even if I already seen the island, I scanned the water like Kwai Chang Caine in the desert lookin for baddies wi his wee narrow eyes. I scan the water so I can spot the island an show it to Gal. He probably seen it too. That'll be why he flopped at this bit. But some things ye've just got to do when ye're out wi yer pal. An Gal's ma pal – no doubt about that.

I points.

Gal...

Gal springs up an does the same Kung Fu look. Rotatin his head till his eyes click on the island. See! He knows that's where the Moorhen's is. I know that too but it's not ma job. He's got to spot it or the whole shebang's upside down.

He starts takin his clothes off without movin his stare off of the island. Should've seen him. Never fumbled a button an before ye can say Bobby Washable Jeans he's nood.

Keep the edge up for Mackenzie, he goes steppin out his Y's an nearly fallin in. I gets his gear thegether.

Some man. STILL doesn't turn round. Ma head's birlin checkin for Mackenzie an anybody that might not like Gal in the nood.

Yeeeeuck! He's paddin in an black gunge squeezes through his toes like the way ye squeeze mince an tatties through yer teeth at yer sister to put her off. So ye can get her dinner. Ye can hear it fartin under his feet an skitterin up through his toes.

He's lookin direct ahead. Right where the nest must be. Inchin into black mirror water. Not lookin back. He's reflected the sact same below. It's like his legs're gettin shorter all the time. Like he's walkin into a statue of hiself. If he kept goin it'd just be hair on the top an hair under the water. A ball of fur – or a hedgehog that's floatin by.

The water reaches his willie an he turns an shivers. I hate that. Like when yer maws took ye on the blue train to Helensburgh an yees're all on the beach. Soon as the rain stops some eejit goes in the water. *Trunks on!* shouts the maws. Next thing ye're freezin. Shiverin behind an aul tore towel. Yer knees hittin like clackers an mibbi tryin to stuff all yer fingers in yer mouth. So then ye'd need to paddle in to show yer da ye were tough.

Worst bit's when it reaches yer willie – *BRRRRRRRR-RRRRRRRRRRRR* – that's what they say in the *Beano*. *BRRRRRRRRRRRRRRRRRRRR* – They're right there. That's sactly the noise ye make. An when ye turn there's yer maw an da an all yer aunties laughin. Like the Doctor White Supers I was on about before.

But I'm not laughin at Gal when he turns round. Some things ye don't need to say an water reachin yer willie is somethin ye never need to say.

Oh excuse me Gal old bean isn't it really cold when the water reaches yer privates?

Yes Derrick old friend – I'm glad you know that too.

Not Gal. No way he's goin to mention it. He takes a deep breath an dives in an commandos at the island. I feels dead proud. I've even forgot Mackenzie. Gal's glidin just below the surface. It's his pink skin surrounded by jet black water. It's like a paintin. His head comes up. He takes a big *Beano* GULP an then he slooshes back till it's only streamers of his hair draggin along the top of the water. Then up comes his head again. GULP. Great. Magic.

Most of the times ye've got to think about somethin to shout but this time I shouts without thinkin anythin.

Alf Tupper Tough of the Track Gal! I goes. I says it that loud they must've heard me at the Fountain. Gal waves a bit an swims right up to the nest. He stands up in the water. It's that deep it's just his soldiers stickin up like two tennis balls floatin beside his head.

THIS MOORHEN

flaps out the island. Just as Gal was goin to touch it. I get some fright but Gal's a safebreaker. Calm. Right in no messin. Partin the grass an reeds like the way he always does – wi his knuckles thegether an his palms turned out.

On ye go Gal – best nest hunter in Cadzow.

But after I say that there's this big empty silence. Like the world's remindin me I'm in the Slaggy. An Gal's stuck out in the Burn. I starts hummin Van Der Valk. 𝄞 Doo do do doo

do do do do do doo do do doo do do do doo Doo do do doo
do do do do do doo do do doo do do do doo. If anybody
comes I'll not run. I'll stay here. An they'll be doin me in an
torturin me. Askin all about where Gal's hidin an I'll say
nothin. An Gal'll be behind reeds bitin his lip an mibbi
shuttin his eyes when they're shovin matches up ma nails an
lightin them. But I'll say, *Who's Gal? Never heard of him!* He's
safe wi me the bold Gal. Safe as houses.

Mmmmmmmmmmmmmmmmm, Gal's goin, so I'll know
there's somethin in it. But I'm more interested in who's goin
to burst out the trees any minute. That's what I'm interested
in.

An I'm just bein interested in all that stuff when,

THIS OTHER

MOORHEN flaps out the island.

Christ! Gal's hand must've been right under it. Right in
that warm bit between the bird's stumic an the feathery nest.

I stops runnin before Gal sees I've started an the two
birds're flyin up an down the Burn. Ye should see what they
do. They come at the water like mad jet pilots, an then run
along slappin the surface wi their flippers an then flop in
tightenin up their feathers. They just skid along the surface
till the burble of water on their chests stops them.

Gal's still not carin. He's got his chest on the island now,
balancin. Feelin about. He's rollin eggs against each other. I
can hear the soft click they make – all fragile an heavy.

Hey Gal yer arse is like Sonny Hammil wi a split head.

He bends round at his baldy white arse an laughs. But he
can't laugh right cos his chest's balancin him so he's lettin
out wee queeks. The Moorhens start lookin at him like he's

talkin Moorhen-eese. Noddin away like they agree wi every word he's sayin.

Any in it Gal? I says in the shout whisper he larnt me. The birds draw me a look like I've interrupted their conversation. Gal nods that there's eggs in it. So I gets a good look about. Nothin. He sticks an egg in his gub for the swim back. Well I never seen it was an egg. I mean it could be the nest – or a kangaroo for all I know – but if ye were takin bets I'd bet on an egg. Not a crocodile or the Empire States Buildin.

He's commandoin back over when I sees movin out the side of ma face.

Raaaaaaaaaaaaaaaaaaaaaaaaaaaaaaaaaaat!!!!

Gal looks startled but cos his mouth's shut tight he looks like him out the *Carry On* films. Kenneth Millar. Gal's da says they're all poofs.

Maw what's Poofs?

SALAP. *Pat ye want to hear the language of this laddie!*

Gal says they're two men that kiss each other.

EEEEUCH!

Ma grannie's got a wee round seat called a Poofy. I'm not sittin on it again. But anyway. This big rat's comin at Gal – whooshin along at the point of this big triangle.

Swim Gal! Swim like fuck!

None of yer commando head up GULP head down glidin through the water this time. No sir. It's splash splosh splash an white foamy water. He hates rats. He's a windmill comin through the Burn. His arms're twenty feet long an his hands're kitchen doors. The only thing holdin him back's his ears.

He sees the rat comin right at him. The rat screws its eyes up an gives an extra wee dig at the water. Swear.

I'm lookin for stones to stoat off its wee blinkin eyes an Gal's splashin furious towards the bank. The rat's that close I'd probably scud Gal. I'm tryin to get him ashore by pressin ma two wrists in ma belly an noddin ma head an the whole top of ma body back an forward an poppin ma eyes out.

I pulls him out. The rat whizzzzzzzzzzzzzzzzzzzzzzzzzzzez by an dunts it's head in the mucky bank wi a skweek. Idiot.

It's gone. The water's still. We launch a few stones where we think it's hidin.

Weird – when we calm down there's me in all ma clothes an Gal's nood. He wiggles his arse side to side so his shrivelled up wullie's hittin one leg then the other. It's the funniest thing ever.

That's a pisser Gal, I says.

But he doesn't laugh. He doesn't laugh cos he's got this egg in his mouth. He shoves it out. He's like a witchdoctor nood wi an egg on his tongue. Ye'd think I'd remember all about Gal bein nood but that's not it. I remember the egg. It's the same colour as a stone an there's freckles. Ma first Moorhen's. It's balanced on his tongue like the only thing in the world.

That's some egg Gal so it is. You're the best nest hunter ever Gal. The Best. So he smiles an takes it out his mouth an puts it between his thumb an pointin finger. That's the way ye hold an egg.

Is it cloakin Gal?

Naw.

How'd'ye know?

Just laid.

How'd'ye know?

Only four in it.

So?

Moorhens lay fifteen – so they must've just started.

That's why that wummin one skelped the water – right hard – full up wi eggs.

Eh? he goes, holdin the egg up to the light.

Nothin, I says, but he's not listenin anyway. All I was sayin is that the wummin Moorhen must still have ten in her belly. No wonder she never wanted to leave the nest! Ever tried to go runnin after the Christmas Dinner at School? Sactly!

Gal's inspectin the egg. So's the maw bird. She thinks Gal's not goin to touch it. She thinks he's goin to put it back. I think she likes us. If we came down every day an fed her an her yunks she'd be tame an we could take her walks up the Street on a wee rope.

Hi Yi Gal Hi Yi Derrick – how's the tame Moorhen gettin on? they'd all go.

Oh just fine, we'd say, *it can beg for chips,* an   KER-ROCK KER-ROCK   says the burdie.

The egg's a planet. An Gal's eye's comin round it like another planet an ma eye's comin round like stars. The only thing missin's wee spaceships comin off our eyes an landin on the egg surface.

Beam me up Scottie.

I'll put it back, goes Gal after ages.

I'm thinkin RAT but I'm not wantin him to know. But when I look at Gal wi ma ordinary not thinkin Rat look – he's scannin the water for the rat. We don't need to say nothin sometimes.

He starts singin.

🎼 *Ben the two of us need look no more.*
We both found what we've been lookin for...

Well! The two of us walk about like half-shut knifes laughin. I mean that Michael Jackson never met a rat in his life if he thinks they're the best thing since square sausages. Christ! Even Oor Wullie knows rats is bad.

Jings maw geez ma tatties n mince me n Fat Boab got chased the day wi a rat. Down the stoorie burn. Where's ma buckit?

There was rats, rats as big as army cats in the store! ma maw always sings an goes on about these rats the size of elephants by the time she's finished. They lived in the walls in the Slap Up. That's where she lived. It's all these houses that got slapped up an if me an Gal think we've got it bad now well we should've seen the way they lived in them days. One pint of milk between the whole street. Blah blah blah. *Lived in a shoebox in the middle of the road,* Gal says.

Everybody knew rats was bad news. Except for Michael Jackson. Weirdo.

After we laugh our heads off we bend down an pick the heads up – only kiddin! After we're finished laughin Gal puts the egg back in his mouth an slides in the water. He does commando again seein as how the rat might be listenin somewhere. Mibbi chewin away on a baby's ear. The rats in the Slap Up used to go in the wane's cot an rip off an ear an take it home for supper. *First ye knew about it is when ye looked at the wane an there's somethin different but ye just can't make it out,* ma da says.

Gal's swimmin back an I'm keepin a sharp look out for Mr Rat. Nothin. Funny – every time it's quiet all the other noises ye don't usually listen to stick right out. The birds. The water. The wind in the trees. An the Water Hens – they're flappin an jumpin out the water an splashin back in. Havin a wee party cos the egg's gettin put back.

Everythin's great. But it's the Slaggy remember. Gal's on his way over to the nest an the birds're chuffed. That's how what happened next wasted that bit of the day.

Gal's halfway to the nest an the Moorhens're sittin in the water wi their arms folded – probably tappin their wee webbed feet under water. Waitin.

I sees this shadow movin behind the trees. It's not

Mackenzie cos he's always clumpin about wi Docs an yella laces.

I trace this thing to a tree. I look over at Gal cos I'm goin to tell him this time. I never sayed about Strangler Joe an it was too late. Nearly. But he's still swimmin so I don't bother.

I walks towards the bush. I've got this bit of rusty washin machine.

Gal's balanced on his chest at the nest again.

I gets right next to the bush an there's somethin movin for sure. I'm thinkin I'll just thunder the bush a few times wi the washin machine bit. But then I thinks what if it's a wee boy an I kill him. So I shoves the metal thing in ma teeth an puts ma hands in the way Gal does. I'm standin there wi ma hands in the heart of the bush. I've not separated the branches yet but I can feel whatever it is twitchin through the twigs into ma body. Like when a fish is on yer fishin rod.

See me? Sometimes I can't tell what I'm goin to do next. I decide not to open the bush an walk back to the Burn. I do that all time now. If it's somethin bad I kid it's not there. I block it out ma mind wi somethin else. Gigantor's good for that. But this time as I'm walkin away I imagines I hears ma da's voice. An he's not talkin he's singin. Rockin Rollin Ridin. That's the song. I'm about to turn back to the bush but Gal's got the egg in the nest an he's up to his soldiers checkin for the rat.

Alf Tupper! he shouts an plunges in. It's not commando. Windmill.

The Moorhens're poppin about the nest gettin settled back in for the night. They're drawin us looks an glad we're gone.

Hope there's no more visitors the night Mrs Moorhen.

Me too Daddy Moorhen – turn the Moorhen Telly on dear? Bill an Ben the Flowerpot Moorhens're on.

No No dear they're not on the telly any more.

Rat's away home – listen to its Michael Jackson LP probably. *Batty For Rats* or somethin. Or Batty Glitter. Or Alvin Ratdust. Or Donny Osmond an the rest of the rats.

Gal tugs out the water like a labrador. His two soldiers're pressin against his ears before he heaves up. He flings on his gear an off we pop wi him tuggin at his clothes cos they're stickin to him. I hate that.

Funny thing is – I looks back at the bush an in the darkness I thought I saw a face. But it's not any aul face. It's ma da's face. That's when I knew ma head's really away wi it. What's ma da's face goin to be doin out there in the middle of a bush in the middle of the Slaggy? Christ – he can hardly get to the telly an back without stoppin for half an hour's rest.

Hansel an Gretel

We're right in the Slaggy now.

Down! Gal goes an falls grabbin the pocket of ma jeans.

He presses his lips tight an points down the hill.

All I see is this hole in the ground below the Pipe. Then who pops his head out but Septic. We're right in the grass spectin Mackenzie. Septic's in an out this hole lookin about like he's got a spring for a neck.

No Mackenzie. Septic's too spicious. Know what he's doin? Bringin out swedger boxes an Fag boxes an emptyin them in a jumper wi knots tied in the sleeves. Then he puts the empty boxes back in the hole.

I gives Gal one eyebrow.

He gives me two eyebrows.

He's stealin Mackenzie's stuff. Septic's knickin off of Mackenzie. Jee-sus!

Me an Gal sometimes do the same thing at the same time. Like twins. I turns an makes this wee tunnel wi ma lips an blows out. It's one of them faces that says I'm glad that's not me stealin Mackenzie's swedgers. Gal's doin the sact same face at the sact same time. Mackenzie catchin ye stealin his stuff! That'd be the worst thing ever. Worse than tellin Mad Wilma about the sluggie.

Septic does a donnybrook wi the tied sleeve jumper over his shoulder. But this bag falls out an he doesn't notice. Septic rattles into the trees.

I gives Gal two eyebrows.

Gal gives me one eyebrow.

C'mon, he goes an scoots down the hill.

It's Flyin Saucers. A big bag. They're made out communion. Two bits stuck thegether an filled wi Sherbet Dip fizz.

Gal's first. Stuffin them in his gub. We're foamin at the lips like two dogs wi rabies. I love fizz. It's a wee ball of electric buzzin round yer tongue. Wi skite some at the Moorhens. Probably be bubblin away all night. Dribblin all over the place.

Munch munchity munch we go off into the woods. There's this trail of Sherbet Dip fallin from our mouths. Fizzy Hansel an Gretel – that's me an Gal. We'll be able to lick our way home along thin lines of fizz. Even in the dark.

Anyway, we're twistin round trees not doin anythin. We're great at that me an Gal. Sometimes we go for years without doin nothin an then we do millions of things. There's no tellin wi me an him. No tellin at all.

Gal pokes me. *Shhhhhhhhhhh,* he goes, an nods across the Burn. He's on his hunkers pullin his sling out his back pocket. All the time his pointin finger's locked on this space.

Somethin's movin. A squirrel scratchin its cheek wi its back leg. Or a dog. Just when I sees what it really is Gal holds out a selection of ball bearins. *Bernie – The Bolt,* he goes.

I puts this big shiny thing in the wee leather cradle. I can see me an him an all these green trees bendin over the curvy mirror. An the tops of the hills white in the background. It's like the whole world's pressed into that wee ball. Gal levels the sling up. The two of us're on our hunkers now an Gal's got a straight line right through to Mackenzie.

This big bit of sun's just lut him up. Star of the show. Doesn't know we're watchin. Sometimes ye can't be sure if somebody knows if ye're watchin. Or not watchin. I mean, they might be lookin the other way an kiddin on they can't see ye when all the time they're skwintin out the side of their eye.

But this time I definitely knew Mackenzie didn't see us. An Gal knew Mackenzie didn't see us. Definitely. Know how we knew that? Cos he's pullin his puddin. There's a lot of names for it. Gal knows them all. Pullin yer wire. Chuggin it. Slappin it. Chokin the Bishop. But to cut a long story shorter Mackenzie's havin a wank. The catalogue. Member? He's pullin away wi his right hand an flickin pages back an forward wi his left. Wimmin's underwear. I mean – I know now – Gal got his maw's catalogue out. Wow! Right after wimmin's shoes – Knickers, bras, tights, stockins, suspenders, an all these other things ye liked.

But that was the first I ever heard about pullin yer wire wi a catalogue. In fact me an Gal'd only just got learnt wanks. Danny Garrett showed us.

This day we're down the Oil Pond to catch frogs. There's millions. Usually ye've to hunt in the reeds all day an ye might get two. Three sometimes. But this day there's half a million. All stuck thegether. Doin carry codes. That's carryin somebody like coal. It's no use easy. Yer jar's brimmin too quick. Me an Gal's sittin fed up. Surrounded by frogs.

Know what they're doin? goes Danny Garrett.

Me an Gal's bored.

Know what they're doin? Eh do yees? goes Danny again wi this voice that never wanted nobody else to hear it.

Carry codes, says Gal an spins one back in the water by the leg.

Danny Garrett laughs. *Carry codes!* He goes. Then he says it again. *Carry codes!* Then he says it a couple of other times. Then he says it like a question. *Carry codes? Are you daft or what?*

He laughs in Gal's face. Like Beryl the Peril when it's only her mouth an jumper lookin out the comic. Gal leans back an

waves his palm about in front of his nose. Death breath
Danny's got. But he keeps on laughin the Garrett fella.

They don't know what it is, he keeps tellin the reeds an
frogs. *They don't know what it is!!*

Eventually he shuts his geggie. Peace.

We birl some more frogs in an start headin home.

But he's dead set on bringin these carry code frogs back
up. Me an Gal ignore him. There's somethin not right about
the whole thing. What's so special about a couple of smelly
aul frogs divin about on each other's backs? Nothin – that's
what.

So he stops bringin it up. It's hot. There's wavy bits of
sunlight just above the ground. We're dossin through the
woods lookin for good nests.

Down! goes Danny. There's this man an wummin. He's
lyin on top of her an she's wrigglin about. We're
bellyflapped. Might not be good at much sept takin his maw
her pills but Danny Garrett can bellyflap. Me an him an Gal
bellyflap right up. They're breathin like they've just got
away from the Polis. He's slabberin all over her an she's
swingin her head from side to side. I don't think she likes it.
He's chewin her neck like a hungry alsatian, Gal says. He's goin
C'mon C'mon, all the time like he tryin to get a Mars Bar off
her – or a box of whoppers.

But she's goin *No no,* an groanin. She hates it. *How does she
not get up an run Gal?* I goes. Her blouse is open. Ye can
nearly see her diddies. Next thing the guy's shovin his hand
up her skirt

I pops up an says, *Excuse me but I can nearly see her diddies!*
Aye! So an I did! Right yar! But I wanted to see them.

Danny Garrett's on his belly an it's like me an Gal's not
there. His eyes're poppin out an his arm's goin like a fiddler
under his body. He starts gruntin. First it's piglet grunts –
then he gets louder an louder. I nudges Gal but he's too busy

memorisin the wummin's knickers cos she's pullin them up an the man's pullin them down.

Tug

                                                                    Tug

Tug

                                                                    Tug

Now Danny Garrett's gruntin like a aul sick dog. The man can hear somethin. I sticks ma hand over Danny's mouth.

Fuck off! he goes dead loud.

Well that's it. The wummin flings the man off an pulls her blouse criss cross. The man sits up wi eyes like missiles on him – starin. He probably sees three wee guys. One wi his hand on his tadger. One wi his hand on his mouth an one wi his eyes on the wummin's knickers.

Not last night but the night before three wee monkeys came to ma door one wi a fiddle one wi a drum an one wi a pancake stuck to its bum. That's goin round in ma head just before the man picks up a stick.

Ten seconds an we're dodgin rocks across the Burn. Soaked. Last I see is the wummin's headin across this golden field an the man's pullin her back. She's got the same folded arms yer maw's got shoutin at ye.

We get in these other trees an get the gear off sept the Y's. We're sunbathin. The wet gear's hangin over trees. The water's drippin off an hittin the grass. The blades're bendin an springin back up an flingin the drops of water away. Hunners of them. All movin about like wee green dancers in the spotlight of the sun.

I feel like a wank, says Danny Garrett.

I thinks – magine slaggin yerself.

Ye look like a wank too, says Gal. Sactly what I was goin to say. I can't figure out how he's callin hiself a wank.

Gal's brothers called us it all the time.

Ya pair of wankers, they'd go. Up to the carry code frogs I thought a wank was ye were daft. Like trippin over the pavement. Or openin yer cheese an onion at the bottom.

I'm lookin at the blue sky. I've got a big straw in ma mouth. I'm like in films. I can hear the Burn an animals thuddin about. The straw's curvin up to the sun an the sun's cookin us nice an slow. Nice an slow. The leaves're shiverin green then blindin an the birds're hoppin from branch to branch. The branches're bendin a bit wi this soft kerrashshshshshshsh. Sometimes the odd white cloud evaporates – like a hole in the blue sky gettin patched up. Gal's pickin away at the grass.

I'm havin a wank, goes Danny Garrett. It's like his voice is miles away.

Me an Gal lean up an look at each other. I don't know if Gal never knew what a wank was but he never let on it if he did.

Danny gets his willie in his hand an starts pullin it away from him then back. The wee smooth bit's peekin out then disappearin. It was nothin really but somethin's sayin don't mention this to yer maw or Father Boyle. It's durty. I'm amazin. I knew wankin was durty before I knew how to do it.

Danny Garrett's gettin faster an faster.

I looks up at the sky an so does Gal cos Danny Garrett's sees somethin interestin up there. His eyes go all skwinty.

What ye doin Danny? I goes.

He slows down a bit an brings his eyes out the sky.

Wankin, he goes pullin ma eyes to his hand wi his eyes.

Aye, but what's it for?

What's it for?

He laughs like at the Oil Pond. Gal laughed too – like he knew. But he never. He just never wanted to look daft. I never says nothin about it.

When Danny Garrett stops laughin I says,

I don't know what it's for.

He looks like he thinks we're takin the piss out him now.

Ye don't know what a wank is?

Me an Gal nod. Only I'm noddin no an Gal's noddin aye.

Danny gives it the look yer da gives ye when he's goin to show ye to tie a fishin knot or balance the wheel on yer bike.

Right, he goes – take yer dicks out.

Me an Gal take our dicks out.

Do this, an he starts doin what he was doin before.

It's tickely.

So there's the three of us goin like trains in this wee clearin. Choockity choo chookity choo Choockity choo chookity choo Choockity choo chookity choo Choockity choo chookity choo Choockity choo chookity choo.

Faster an faster we're gettin.

The runaway train came over the hill an she blew hoo hoo, sings Gal.

We've lost the stupit-lookin grins an it's gettin quite good.

Danny's back lookin at the sky again an Gal's lookin in the Burn. I looks at a tree.

Danny moans out like he's just been clubbed to death wi a caveman. His top lip's shovin itself up his teeth towards his nose.

Gal starts makin his on the Swing noise.

Whooooooooooheeeeeeeeeeeeeee!

Next thing the biggest tickely feelin ever

rushes along the grass an sweeps right through me.

Magic. Fuckin magic! Me an Gal look at each other. It's like the best egg times a million. Like the Swing plus jumpin off the Pipe.

So I looks at Danny an he's rubbin his off these leaves. It's all white stuff.

What's that?

Spunk.

Me an Gal look at our willies. Danny looks at our willies an shakes his head.

Youse won't get that yet.

Oh! we goes, an gets the gear back on. An that's it. First wank. Me an Gal wanked every chance we got after that. I'm still doin it. It's great. First thing in the mornin was,

D'ye have a wank?

Aye.

D'ye get the Feelin?

Aye!

An we'd walk away smilin.

I love the Feelin. Great.

Then Gal stopped talkin about it. I thought he'd forgot. Every time I asked him if he had a wank last night he changed the subject. So it was one of the things ye never talked about.

Christ there I'm away all over the shop again. I was tellin ye about Mackenzie havin a wank this time. Because Danny Garrett learned us we knew sactly what Mackenzie was doin.

Mackenzie's big pink arse is starin right at us. Spotty.

Look – Sonny Hammil wi a split head, goes Gal an takes aim.

Up a bit, left a bit, down a bit – FIRE, I'm goin.

He fires.

WHISSSSSSSSSSSSSSSSSSSSSSSSSSSSSSSSSSSSSSSSSSSSSSSSSSSSS

Right up Mackenzie's arse! A ball-bearin! This long silver streak's goin through the air:

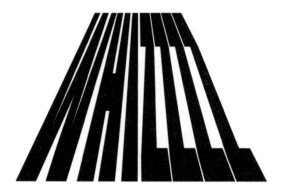

an ye're spectin a skelp but it's a quiet thud – a thid really an

ARGHGHGHGHGHGGH!!!!!!!!

says Mackenzie jumpin up. He doesn't know to run or pull up his trousers or rub his arse.

> Man
> we
> are
> in
> knots

in the grass.

Gal's bitin ma soldier an Mackenzie's screams're flyin over the Burn an over us like low-flyin jets.

Mind I sayed we were good at bellyflappin? Well there's somethin else we're good at too – backwards bellyflappin. Ye'd've thought we were a film goin backwards the way we slid through the long grass an in the trees before we went to hunkers.

But he's not called SAS Mackenzie for nothin ye know. He spots the trees movin.

Gal's loadin the sling. No Bernie the Bolt this time. It's in case Mackenzie charges. Wi his strides round his ankles but?

No chance. His Willie's swingin about like an elephant's trunk lookin for buns. It looks like it never liked the interruption. Not one bit.

Me an Gal's holdin breaths an he pulls his trousers up gruntin when they get to where the ball-bearin went. Then what does the bold Gal do?

ZzzzzzzzzzzzzzZZZZ**zzzzzz**lingngngngng

WHACK!!!

Perfect. Right on the forehead. But Mackenzie doesn't even go one step backwards. No sir. Not him. Splashes right in the Burn. Starts wadin. Shoutin the odds about goin to chop us up in bits. His mouth's this black hole openin an shuttin in the green trees an the white hills an the glassy burn. An his arms're wavin about an pointin like they're angrier than the rest of him.

But we're sharp me an Gal. Never mind backwards bellyflappin an sideways bellyflappin – what about sideways backwards bellyflappin? We've backwards bellyflapped sideways an he's shoutin at the wrong bit. He's chuckin rocks at the bit we used to be a minute ago.

Ya fuckers. I'll get yees. Youse're fuckin dead. D'ye hear me? Dead! Mackenzie's shoutin. He's nearly blowin the trees over wi his voice. Then he's rubbin his sore arse an the water's runnin out him. I'm always sayin that now. Arse. I used to say bum all the time but I say arse now. It's nearly swearin that. Arse. So it is. I don't say arse to ma maw an da but. Magine it?

Hey da, I'll just sit here on ma arse an eat ma tea.

SCUD!

A boot up the arse's what I'd be gettin for that carry on. But I'm sayin arse now instead of bum cos that's me started second year.

Mackenzie's lookin for a movin leaf or a twig snappin. Or mibbi just a wee bird flappin an givin him the nod – *There they're there Mackenzie! Tweet Tweet!!* Pointin the tip of its wing. A peek at a face or a jumper an we're dead for the rest of our lifes. I'm not movin like anythin. I think Gal's stopped as anythin too. That's why I thinks *mad* when Gal sings. A song about wankin. Well not really wankin. It's about the Feelin. I like it. It's funny. But I don't want him singin it at Mackenzie just cos it's funny. Specially wi the ball-bearin up his arse.

𝄞*Does yer dick hang low?* Gal goes in a different voice.

Like his Lizzie.

KERRRRRRRRRRRRRRRRRRRRRRASH

Mackenzie launches a rock at the voice.

There's   this   quiet.

Ye can feel Mackenzie's ears doin bat radar in the tree gaps. The birds're even listenin. Then Gal sings the next line.

𝄞*Does it wobble to an fro?*

Mackenzie's not got a scooby cos it's bouncin off all the trees an over the Burn at all different bits.

Baaaaaaaaaaaaaaaaaaaaaaaaastard!!!!!!!!!!!!!!!

says Mackenzie an launches another rock.

KERRRRRRRRRRRRRRRRRRRRRRRASH

I know who ye are – ye're dead. Hear me? Dead.
He goes.

There's more silent. Our soldiers're four jellies on the Jackson Street bus. The birds're whistlin at the quiet an lookin for an answer. Gal goes,

𝄞*Do ye ever get the feelin that it's bouncin off the*

ceilin?

KERRRRRRRRRRRRRRRRRRRRRRRRASH

A close-for-comfort lands right at Gal's voice. Gal lets out this scream like it's his head an we start backwards zig zaggin bellyflappin fast.

ARRRGHGHGHGHGHGHGHGHGH!!!!!

Oh Ya – ooh ya – right on the head. Mammy! Mammy! Ma head. Ma head.

Mackenzie's a big happy grin. Man it's like the sun's comin across the field to me an Gal. But Gal wiped his Colgate smile off wi a Woody the Woodpecker.

Ha ha ha haaaaaaaaaaa ha

Ha ha ha haaaaaaaaaaa ha

His face fell like half a paper plate flyin down into the Burn an gettin washed away. Well! It's a right laugh now. Gal gives it laldy. I'm shoutin Mackenzie after every line Gal sings.

Does yer dick hang low?

MACKENZIE!

Does it wobble to an fro?

MACKENZIE!

Do ye ever get the feelin,

MACKENZIE!

that it's bouncin off the ceilin?

MACKENZIE!

It's more shoutin than singin.

Mackenzie   goes   **bal**   istic. It's us knowin his name that does it. He's splashin about liftin piles of big chuckies.

That's it. That's it. Ye're fuckin dead. Hear me. I know who ye are. I know yer voice.

He's throwin chuckies in the trees. They're that smooth they don't birr. Ye only hear them when they scud. Or hit a tree. Or when it's a big blue flash in yer head.

The stones're landin away nowhere near us. We bellyflap back the way we came till Mackenzie's screamin is just a dog yelpin far away. Off we pops huntin for nests.

It's ages an we're thinkin everythin's alright when

Whooooooooooooooooooooooooooooooooosh

ma heart's got a mouth an Gal's fingers're diggin in. Mackenzie's ten feet in front of us.

Plop we're eatin dirt. Peekin through our eyebrows. Breathin worm world. *Hey! Fuck off! That's our air yer breathin,* the worms're goin.

Mackenzie's where Septic took the swedgers an fags. He's pullin empty boxes out the hole an flingin them over his soldiers.

Bastard! Fuck! Shit! He's goin. Me an Gal's soldier jellies again. But I'm feart too like the Burn's runnin through ma back an out ma belly.

Mackenzie stands up strokin his chin the way teachers an doctors do it. Or people on the telly about paintins. *It helps ye to think,* ma da says, *they've got their brain in their chins – that's them clappin it.*

BING!

Mackenzie gets a good idea.

Well – a good idea for him but a bad idea for me an Gal.

He rubs his arse an ye can tell he thinks it's the same people that shot his arse that stole his stuff. All he needs to do now is find out their names.

He pulls out his big knife an starts cuttin the boxes up. Not mad an wild like ye'd spect any normal mad guy. No. Not Mackenzie. Not SAS Mackenzie. He slices them slow. An if boxes can feel these ones went through some torture so they did. Some torture.

Hank Marvin

We backwards sideways zigzag bellyflap away an bolt the course home. Starvin.

I'm Hank Marvin, goes Gal.

Me too. Lee Marvin.

I could eat a scabby horse in a folded over mattress, he says.

I could chew the tyres off a bus. Movin.

I could juggle rabbits on ma tongue.

I could...

I could dip ma piece in a split head.

I could...

I could eat ma grannie's wooden leg.

I could...

He had the best patter Gal. I never liked gettin beat usually but it was OK off of Gal. Gal was goin to grow up an have the best patter in Cadzow – mibbi the Brig even.

When Gal gets in I hears Maw Gal shoutin an bawlin.

Have you been in that effin Burn? An look at them hands – ye're not sittin down to yer tea wi hands the colour of Anniker's Midden...

SALAP! Right in the kisser he gets it. He lets out the same scream as when he jags hiself wi a thorn.

Then his da gets it. Usual.

An you ya bastard pishin the Giro up the wall! That's all ye're good for. Yer mother was right ya durty stinkin good for nothin alky.

A couple of plates smash. Then there's nothin. Then the windae opens where I'm listenin. I've got to move. Quiet.

A hand – pink an purple wrinkles – empties a bottle of Buckie in the garden. Just misses me. It smells like the pub. Or Big Gal's breath. There's this rose tree growin there. It's great. The rest of the garden's a right tip. The Addams Family Rose Garden, Mrs Murphy calls it. She's got a good mind to phone the council.

...a no good alky! Maw Gal shouts. She shouts it like the end of a sentence. But she's not been shoutin. It's only half a sentence she's sayin. Mibbi she forgets what she's sayin an just says half the words. That's probably why Big Gal can't make out what she's sayin. Mibbi she says half it in her head an half it out loud. I'm bored soon so I vault in ma own bit.

So I'm in the scullery talkin to ma maw's bum. Ma maw's like that wummin on Tom an Jerry. Ye only ever see her bum. She's clickin plates an pots in the sink. I think she puts cups an stuff in there to click just for the sake of it. She's always at it – an singin – that's what she's always doin. She could go on the telly.

Good evenin ladies an gentlemen. Welcome to the GALDERRICK show. An tonight we've got Derrick Daniel Riley's maw – the Incredible Singin Bum.

She's some singer ma maw right enough, even Gal says it. Even Gal's maw says it this day to Big Gal. *She's a great singer Derrick's maw so she is. Some singer. Aye. Yer mother can sing. Hey Gal – Gal that Alice so she can sing...* she went on an on an on an on an on about it man as if it was a rocket to the moon.

So when I walks in the scullery I thought she was singin her favourite – 'I once had a dear old mother'. She always sings it an when she's finished we dive on her an slabber her wi kisses. When she's got us in the right mood she goes,

Who wants to scratch ma back?

Me Maw! Me Maw! an they dive in behind her an start clawin away.

Who want's to pick the Belair out ma hair?

Me Maw! Me Maw! an in goes somebody else pickin away.

Who wants to pick ma corns?

Me Maw! Me Maw!

Couldn't get near her for clawin an scratchin an pickin. An all them Me Maw's was like Invasion Of The Fire Engines. Get it? Me Maw Me Maw? It's a Joke. This Fireman goes in an his maw shouts *who's that?* an he goes, *It's Mee Maw, Mee Maw*. That's the joke.

I suppose ye want to know it in case ye want to try it out. It's a right weepie. All ma sisters cry when they hear it...

I once had a dear old mother
who was awful kind to me.
And when I was in trouble
she sat me on her knee.

One day as I lay sleeping
in my little feather bed.
An angel came from heaven
and told me Mum was dead.

I woke up in the morning
to see if it was true.
My mum had gone to heaven
above the sky so blue.

So children obey your parents
and do as you are told.
For if you lose your mother
you lose a heart of gold.

But that's not what she's singin this day. It's another one.
Her voice's vibratin cos the spinner's on in the twin tub.

𝄞*Say g oo oo oo oo bye ye ye my y y own nnnn true lo o o o ver*

DiiiiinnnnnerrrrrzzzzzOnnnnnnn the ta a a ble.

𝄞*This is is is will be ee ee ee our la a a a ast goo oo oo ood bye*

I lifts ma plate an heads out. Kraft cheese dinner an chips.
But ma feet're skweltchin an her ears're twitchin in ma
direction. She's movin towards me.

𝄞*For the carnival is over*
I will love you till I die.

She marches out into the lobby an slaps me on the dish.
Aaawch.

What the hell have I told you about playin down that Burn?

Cos I've got ma plate I'm rubbin ma face off ma soldier
tryin to think of a good answer.
I can't rem...

SALAP!

What have I told ye?
Well! That was enough. I puts the plate down an shoves
ma fists in ma sides like Bugs Bunny an goes in a right posh
voice,
You really have to stop slapping my dish mother – I'm such a
good boy after all! I wasn't near the Burn.

Ma maw smiles an shakes her head. An magics the most amazin cake out thin air.

Oh that's fine then. Would you like another piece of Mr Kipling son? They're exceeeeeeeeeeeeeeeeeeedingly good.

I stretch out an take this enormous slice of fancy cake.

Ma maw growls.

I smile.

She frowns.

I smile.

She slaps me a belter an the cake flicks sideways like Muhammad Ali's gumshield.

I'm back to reality an she's windin her arm up for another slap an shoutin. See ma magination. Sometimes I don't know what's happenin.

An don't go near that Burn again. There's a nutcase escaped out Carstairs. An yer da's took another wee turn an all. He's goin to have to go into a tent.

A tent? I thinks. What good's a tent goin to do him? Me an Gal were in a tent once. We were in his back garden campin out. But his Jim stole it in the middle of the night an took it down the dump an burnt it. First we knows about it is we wakes up an all there is above us is the sky. I looks up an no tent. An there's his Jim at his room windae watchin us an laughin his head off.

But when I asked ma maw she says that wasn't the kind of tent it was. First she looks like she's goin to cry. Then she hits me a soft slap but she's laughin a bit an there's a tear comin down her cheek. I can't make it out sometimes so I can't.

I skwint at the Sacred Heart. *Wimmin! Who needs them?* I goes.

Well! What does the bold Jesus do but wink out one of them blue eyes of his. I looks at ma maw but she never seen it.

I gives Jesus a spicious stáre an jooks in the kitchen.
What's all that noise out there? ma da croaks.
Nothin.
Grunt.

It's the News as usual an ma da's two hands stickin round the paper. His fingers look glued to the edges. Like fingers out the joke shop. He's got a load of pills an medicine in brown bottles on the table. An a load of fluffed up pillows at his back. He coughs that much now ye forget he's coughin. The two bars're on on the fire.
Cost a bloody fortune! says ma maw. *I'm goin to petition for gas.*
Right there! says Maw Gal an on an on they go about the price of most things. Except Doctor White Supers.

Ma da starts askin me about what I've been up to theday. I only tells him about the Moorhen. *A Moorhen's eh,* he goes like it's a precious jewel, *I always wanted one of them. A Moorhen's – that's a good egg right enough. I mind...*

But he's out of breath an he can't talk any more. That's when he does two different things. He reaches out an there's this hissin noise. An when I look up he's got this mask like a spitfire pilot only ye can see through it.

Tss Hisss
Tss Hisss
Tss Hisss

He's takin gulps of air. He turns the black knob on a can beside him again an Pshhhhhht it's off. That's when he reaches under the bed an brings out the wooden box where he keeps his egg collection. He showed me an Gal it once. Me an Gal searched the whole house but never found it. He gives me it. *Here son this is for you,* he says. I open it slow an the hinges squeak. The inside's red velvet. An there's a Ptargamin's an a Hawk's an a Hooded Crow an all kinds of egg – a Spotted Flycatcher – but he's right there's no Moorhen's.

There's no Moorhen's Da, I goes.

He puzzles his eyebrows at me. I holds up the box to him. *Moorhen's – there's none.*

But he's back on the spitfire mask again an he can't hear me. So I closes the box decidin that's what I'll do. I'll go an get him a Moorhen's. Even if I've got to swim out past the rat. I decides to try an cheer him up.

Somewhere there's sunshine Da eh? Somewhere there's rain! Want to sing that? All about the train?

But he only shakes his head an round about his eyes're black.

I'll get ye a Moorhen's Da. Me an Gal's goin back to that nest an we're goin to get the eggs. I'll get one for ye.

On the telly the newsman's tryin to bore me to death. Danny McGowan's got a colour telly. His da's loaded. At night it looks like his house is on fire. First time me an Gal nearly phoned nine nine nine but the phone box was broke. We sneak up an watch it now. But the windae steams up wi our nostrils an sometimes Mrs McGowan pours cups of water on us. She doesn't mean it. She's posh. She says, *Oh my my George this water is mingin I'll just pour it out this here windae.*

Nine times out of ten me an Gal get out the road. Colour tellys're great. Amazin.

Flash in the pan, ma da says. *Bad for yer eyes. Who wants all that colour in the house?*

Me that's who. The man on the news looks at me an grins as if to say, *Here's a special bit of news for you me boy!*

The search tonight continues for...

An he's goin on an on an there's the big baw face of Meccano Joe starin at me. Ma da's still behind the paper breathin an ma maw's in the scullery clickin cups. The rest of them's out or up the stairs playin Tiny Tears.

I looks at ma da's paper an there's big writin sayin.

MODEL MANIAC ENTICES KIDS – KILLS SIX

Ma da turns the page.

AN YOU'RE NEXT DERRICK DANIEL RILEY

The man on the News is still rattlin on about *...on no account to approach Oats – a clinical cyclepath.*

Meccano's face comes back on an winks.

It's lookin at me no matter where I go. Like the Sacred Heart in the lobby.

...Police issued a photofit as Oats might appear without beard and moustache.

But I'm startin to not hear the voice. It's fadin away an these mad eyes're pullin me in like the snake on *Jungle Book – Trutht in me. Jutht in me,* they're goin.

I can't look away. I can't look away. I can't look away. I can't look away. I can't look away. I can't look away. I can't look away. I can't look away. I can't look away. I can't look away. I can't look away. I can't look away. I can't look away. I can't look away.

ARGH!!!!!!!!!!!

Des Dillon

Ma da's

       paper's rustlin

             as I zoom

                  out the kitchen

                       an right up the stairs.

Dreams an Nightmares

I'm lyin on ma bed lookin at this Blackie's through ma magnifyin glass. Well it's half a pair of aul specs really. I'm zoomin in an out. It's like I'm a space ship an the egg's the surface of the planet an I'm comin in for landin. Starship Cadzow here. Captain Riley rekwestin permission to land.

But I looks in ma other hand an instead of a half a pair of aul specs it's this big round Pink Panther magnifyin glass I've got. Inspector Cluedo. When I take the magnifyin glass away there's me an Gal in this ginormous nest wi four eggs the size of beach balls. I smile over at Gal an he smiles back. An there's this right warm feelin rushin up out where ma belly is an I feel great. It's the best place in the world. An Gal's there an that makes it better. A lot better.

We're lyin in this nest. It's made out of sticks an branches. An mud. There's mud holdin it all thegether. But it's not jaggy. There's all these feathers linin the inside where we're lyin. It's the softest stuff ye ever felt in yer life. Ye want to lie there forever it's that comfy. It's like lyin on a cloud. An the tree's swayin gentle side to side an sometimes round in wee smooth circles. It's night but warm wind's feelin our faces. An there's stars everywhere. I looks over at Gal an he smiles. I smile back. Best pals in the solar system. The Universe. The whole world.

His arms're makin a half circle on the edge. I'm the sact same at the other end. An it's up this dead high tree. I mean

HIGH! I put ma feet up at Gal's head an he puts his feet up at mine. It's the way yer Da sticks his on the mantelpiece.

The sky's all sprinkled wi different stars. Red stars. Green stars. Blue stars. White stars. Twinklin an flashin in an out like lights at the Shows. An every time ye want a shootin star

WHOOOOooOooooo

OOOOOOOOOOOSH

There's one goin right across the sky.
First I want one.

WHOOOOooOooooo

OOOOOOOOOOOSH

Then Gal.

WHOOOOooOooooo

OOOOOOOOOOOSH

Then me.

WHOOOOooOooooo

OOOOOOOOOOOSH

An we're laughin at that. Laughin our heads off. Instead of slappin ma thighs I'm slappin the top of this giant egg. It's stone coloured an big brown speckles. Moorhen's.

If ye're out there little spacemen come an talk to us. I'm shoutin it like a nursery rhyme. Gal grins an swings his head back. He's scannin the sky an I can see the million sprinkled stars in miniature on the surface of his eyes. A shootin star traces a line over his eyeballs. For a minute his two eyes look like the white line when ye switch the telly off. An his smile's that big he's the most happy ever. It's the best time ever. The best.

Next minute there's knock knockin an Gal swings his head up. The million stars slide down his cheeks an drag his smile down till he's lookin at me wi these question-mark eyes.

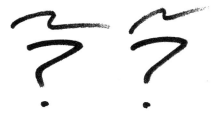

Stars're over the floor of the nest mixin wi the floor like Christmas glitter an tinsel an cotton wool.

Funny thing is when I give him question-mark eyes back he looks at me like he knows what the knockin is. Then he starts laughin. Like a mad maniac. Like it's a great joke an everybody gets it sept me. Like it's about me. Like I'm goin to communion an I've no trousers or Y's on an the whole school's laughin. An Joanne Brennan's there. *Tiddly Tiddly,* she's goin wi a bent pinky an pointin at ma willie. An now the wind's gettin bigger an the nest's blowin about good style. I starts gettin scared. I don't tell Gal cos he's too busy laughin. But his eyes're like dead cats' eyes now.

The tree's swishin from side to side. I hold on tight an looks over the edge. It's a lot higher than it looked a minute ago. But that's not where the knockin's comin from. Gal's still in fits.

Knock knockity knock, it goes again, like a Polis chap. Gal nods at the egg beside me. Christ – that's it – it's the egg. There's a yunk in it an it's chappin tryin to get out. I gives Gal this look. It's a lassies look but it was out before I could stop it. It's the look yer maw an yer sisters do when they meet a pram up the Street.

AAAAAAAAAAAAWWWWWWWWWWWWWWWWWW!!! says ma face an Gal guts hiself.

But it didn't bother me that much cos me an Gal's present at an actual birth!

The egg starts to crack so I move ma ear close. Ye can feel the warmth. Yup – definitely somethin movin in there. More cracks appear like road maps.

A couple of shootin stars go over like they're chasin each other. Wishhh wishhh. This wee hole appears on the shell. Ye can just tell there's a yunk in there peck peckin away. *Right big bad world here I come ready or not in your den by one by two by three,* it's sayin.

I give Gal a big beamin smile an shove ma face right next to it. I'm not missin this for all the horses in China.

So ma face's right on the surface of the egg. Ma nose is pointin right where the hole is. Funny thing is – I think I smell smoke. I looks to see if Gal's found a fag but no.

An just as I put ma face back into lookin position

MACKENZIE'S FACE BURSTS OUT THE EGG!

SMOKIN A FAG

Next thing he's crackin through the shell. The shell's thick as broke dinner plates. All this gooey stuff's holdin him back. Clear stuff, an yella an red. Good job cos he's got his big knife an he's tryin to get a swing at me but the skweeky goo's that thick it's draggin him back like elastic.

I scream an starts clamberin out the nest. I forgot the highness an there's me fallin through the air an all I can hear is Gal screamin for help an Mackenzie slashin into him wi the big blade. An the whizz of the air past ma ears. I can hear that too.

THUD

I hits the ground wi a bang. I'm dead. So I open ma eyes spectin angels wi white wings singin 𝄞*HAAL AY LOO YA*

HAAL AY LOO YA an ma granda an God wi a big book an Our Lady whizzin about on a cloud. But what I see is the ground an grass. An the grass is all swirled round in a pattern. It's dry an rough. More like Bernie's Horse than grass. But it's not grass. It's the carpet in ma room. An there's the half a pair of specs an the Blackie's. The Blackie's is broke.

There's still knockin an I'm lookin round breathin like a lympic runner.

The windae's knockin'. There's this IRA balaclava breathin at the glass. I'm goin backwards like an upside-down crab. An arm comes right in the room an swings the windae open.

Then the hand pulls the mask off.

I stop goin backwards like a demented crab. It's Gal. He's mental so he is. Pure mental.

You're Mental Gal! I goes.

I'm sent for a loaf – comin? he says. But his feet start slippin on the roughcast. I can hear the wee stones pingin off the back shed. The stars in the dream flash back across ma head.

I dives right off the floor an saves him. I felt good cos I left Mackenzie cuttin him up in the dream. I've got his jumper an I'm anchored to the frame wi ma knees.

If I let you go ye're a gonner Gal, I went.

But the bold Gal's never short for answer. *If ye let me drop you're a gonner,* he goes, through his teeth like John Wayne buried in the dirt an German bombs **boomph boomphin** everywhere. Next thing there's barkin. Down below his danglin feet the Manhole Boxer Dog's gnashin away like Gal's feet's dinner. It's got a bandage on its head.

I drags Gal in an we go on about dangerous an ma reflexes an Gal climbin up there in the first place.

The dog reminded us of the time we were in Pender's an Septic came in. Me an Gal stands outside. Septic goes – *Have ye got a bone for the dog?* Pender's bendin into the bone box an Gal leans in an shouts – *Hey Septic – youse gettin a dog!!??*

Pender hunted Septic. *I'm sent for a bone for the dog for the soup,* me an Gal say it all the time now.

So that's what we're talkin about comin back wi the plain Milanda Gal's sent for an who's in the Lane but Septic. Me an Gal could beat Septic but we're feart of Mackenzie. Saves Septic every time that. Nobody'll touch him. Sept Mulligan. He got three years last week an done the Polis in the court in an escaped. He was in the paper. The Record. Still can't find him.

Alf Tupper Tough of The Track, says Gal.

Billy Whizz right at his back, I says, without turnin ma head so Septic never knew we were talkin. We try walkin past but he sticks his two arms out an bumps us thegether.

Mackenzie's goin to kill youse! is the first thing he says. This feelin goes right through me like an electric shock. Like I'm shrinkin away in the pavement cracks.

Us? goes Gal, like Septic was sayin, *Jock Stein wants youse two to play against Rangers this Saturday. Poachers.*

Aye. Goes Septic, *YOUSE,* an he's lovin the fear on our faces. We starts practisin the excuses for Mackenzie on Septic. I'm hopin Septic'll tell the excuses to Mackenzie an he'll say – *Oh that's OK then – I see the picture now – silly aul me thinkin about doin them in. They never done nothin it's all clear to me now.*

Am I daft or somethin? When's Mackenzie ever goin to talk like that. Mackenzie dishes out doins like hot dinners. But we do excuses at Septic anyhow.

But... but... we were gettin chased... an... an...

The Bricklayer...

Rocks were...

It's not the fire.

BANG! That shut me an Gal up. I'm startin to smile cos it's like a big mistake but the smile wipes when Gal gets all fidgety. Septic's lovin it.

Yees stole his gear, goes Septic. Nobody says nothin for a minute. I'm thinkin Gal's goin to say – *We seen you stealin it skwinty!* But he never.

What gear? he goes.

You know what gear!

I don't know what Gal's up to but I decides to keep ma mouth shut.

Your head's puggled Septic. He leans his face into Septic's. *Think we'd be mad enough to mess wi Mackenzie?*

Well he planked his swedgers down the Slaggy an they're not there now.

We never... I goes to say automatic even if I decided to say nothin. That's ma problem ma da says – take ma mouth out on the road before ma head's in gear or somethin. I talk too much. But Gal kicks me. An anyway Septic's Death Breathin Gal – starin in his eyes an round the back gardens at the same time.

He thinks it was youse anyway.

*Blow town! Sure **you** never took them Septic?* Good on the bold Gal. Septic goes chalk white. He's lookin at somethin up the lamp post. For a minute I think he's goin to admit to it.

OK it's a fair cop yees've got me fair an square. Slap the cuffs on an take me down town Kojak Gallacher.

But that's not what he does. *Geez that loaf!* he goes, an grabs the plain Milanda off Gal an starts rippin into it.

He's packin it in wi his bony fingers. Black boggin his fingers are. Ye could grow tatties in his nails. That's what ma maw always says when she's cleanin our ears wi a kirby grip, *Ye could grow tatties in these ears so ye could. Tatties.* Magine! All these long green tattie shaws ropin up out yer ears.

Septic's stuffin his face wi bread an grinnin. Gal moves like to give him a doin. He gives me the c'mon but no way I'm havin Mackenzie killin me for somethin I done. He's already goin to kill us for somethin we never done. Gal spits on the slabs an rubs it in wi his toe. Septic's still tearin lumps of loaf an rammin them in his gub. It minds me of the time me an Gal had this yunk an we couldn't find a nest. We put it in his back shed an fed it three times a day. We had to ram the food down its throat wi a match. It died.

I hate it when I don't know what to do. I look at the grog Gal done on the slabs like I'm readin a book.

Gal's face's fizzin. Septic can't tell but if there's a thing ye learn hangin about wi somebody all yer life, it's when they're fizzin an when they're not fizzin. Gal was fizzin.

Funny thing next. Gal cheers up. Smiles. Well that's what ye'd think if ye were Septic. It was only his face that cheered up. His fists're still tight an his soldiers're tryin to touch his ears. He always done that when he was fizzin – tried to make his soldiers touch his ears. The thing I can't understand is how he's talkin dead nice now to Septic.

Gal puts his arm round Septic's soldier an points up to Sonny Hammil's.

Hey Septic know how Sonny Hammil's mental? he says.

Septic's mouth's tight wi bread. He nods. His slabbers've all dried up an he's still eatin. He scoffed a packet of Cream Crackers without anythin to drink. Know what the bet was? A special fish supper out Krick's. He's lookin up at Sonny Hammil's an squeezin some words out through the dough.

Baldy arsehole, he says. Only it sounds like *Mnaldy Athole.* Sonny Hammil gave him a kickin two weeks ago. Me an Gal seen it. Septic stole his milk. Sonny Hammil jumped all over his legs. *Run now ya wee skwinty bastard,* is what he was shoutin.

We were at his door all night yesterday, says Gal.

Gal uses big wide transmittin eyes. Now I know! It's a plan. I'd nearly forgot about it.

Chap doors run away. He's a Cyclepath, I says, tryin to be Septic's pal too. Me an Gal're learnin stuff like that all the time now. How to kid on ye like somebody when ye don't. Yer maw an da do it all the time. Watch them. *Oh hello Jeanie, nice to see ye,* an she's drawin ma da the that's us in for the night wi this aul cow look.

Gal joins in, *Kept runnin out – howlin at the moon.*

HAAAAAAAOOOOOOOWWWWWWWW

screams Gal at the top of his lungs an runs round kiddin on he's Sonny Hammil. Septic loves it so Gal lays it on thick.

He's lookin up an down the lane like this. Gal's doin the knuckle draggin routine. *OOH OOH OHH!* He's great at that Gal – knuckle draggin. Most people can't do it right but Gal's got long arms an he only needs to bend a wee bit an he's a Griller.

But we weren't there when he came out, says Gal, stoppin right in front of Septic. *OOH OOH!*

Septic gives it question-mark eyes.

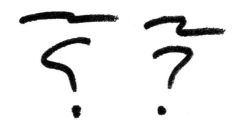

Guess where we were? says Gal, now he's got him hooked.
Dunno???
In the cupboard.
Eh?
The cupboard.

Septic's not got a clue so me an Gal point to these wee cupboards beside the front doors in Cadzow. They're just the right size for me an Gal to squeeze in an shut before Sonny Hammil gets out. They're not for coal nor nothin cos we're all electric. Costs a fortune. No handles either. Ye've to dig yer nails in the corners. Me an Gal's always wonderin about them.

What're they bunkers for out there? I asked ma maw.
That's great son, she goes, *Have you emptied that bin the day?*

Nobody knows. But Septic likes what me an Gal think they're for. For hidin when ye chap doors run away. He's grinnin an the gaps in his teeth're full of Gal's Milanda. Plain.

Ye can see it all filmstrippin on the front of Septic's eyes an the madder Sonny Hammil gets in his head the bigger Septic's smile gets. An the more plain Miranda ye can see. Gal decides to go for it. Now or never. Alf Tupper.

He uses his *I've just had this great idea* voice. But I know it's not really his *I've just had a great idea* voice – it's his *I've just had a great idea* voice wi a wink in it for me. Septic's daft as a brush.

Who says one of us jumps in the cupboard an the other two sees Sonny Hammil's face? Gal goes.

Septic's spicious but Gal's right in before his spicious grows up his head an pulls his eyebrows down.

I'll go up – rattle the door – jump in the cupboard.

Septic likes it. He's noddin like the dog in the back of the car ma uncle Eddie won on Spot the Ball. Ye spot a ball an win a car. Mad. *Spot the Dog,* Gal calls it. Me an Gal's invented Spot the Car. Ye win a ball. Burst. It's in his shed. Gal grabs ma gatepost an kids on he's walkin out the gate. He's whistlin.

You an Derrick come out his gate like yees're goin for a loaf. Like this, an he starts whistlin again doin his gatepost routine. *Ye can whistle any tune ye like.*

Septic's right into it now he's skwintin up at Sonny Hammil's like a Vincent Price.

An Sonny Hammil'll come chargin out like a manic.

Right! goes Septic, but it's only his mouth that says it cos his brain's runnin the filmstrip of what's goin to happen on the inside of his skull.

Gal scoots up the lane. *Chances each!* he shouts over his soldier.

He gives it Alf Tupper without the words. Me an Septic take positions. Gal's bellyflappin across Sonny Hammil's garden. His scullery light's makin a big cartoon colour square on the grass. For a minute I thinks Gal's goin to crawl right in it an get spotted like Stalag Thirteen. But not him. Not Gal. He goes round it like it's concrete an slides up to the door. Me an Septic's got a hand each on the gatepost.

Gal stands up an turns round. He lifts his top lip an shows all his teeth. Then he pulls a bum cheek an makes a fartin noise. Me an Septic's in fits. Bold as brass Gal. But Septic's not daft as ye think. He's scared so he's gettin me between him an Sonny Hammil's.

BANG   CRASH   WALLOP   BOOT KICK PUNCH THUMP SKELP SCUD WHACK THUNDER

Gal murders the door. He's still flippin the letterbox lid an his other hand's openin the cupboard. He's somethin Gal so he is. He's doin all that an he still manages a face down at us.

He's only in the cupboard an Sonny Hammil's in the lane shoutin an rantin.

He spots me an Septic comin out ma gate an givin it innocent walk good style. Blind rage he's in. Like a Dennis the Menace victim.

Did did you see anybody at ma door? Eh! Eh! Did ye? Did ye?

Eh? Some... what...? says Septic, lovin it. Then what does Septic say? When's the van openin Mr Hammil?

Sonny Hammil gives us an evil stare an bolts up the lane wi big clothes-pole legs. Once he's where Gal boots his dog the cupboard opens. Gal sneaks out an vaults the fence. We hides in Murphy's till he goes back in.

It's me now. Gal an Septic're at the gatepost an I'm sneakin up to the door. I crossed the garden an snuck along the wall cos he watches out the scullery sometimes. I'm terryfied. I can smell the night comin in.

I give it the best smile I can down at they two. I don't fart or nothin. Gal gives me the fist in the air. That makes me a bit better but not as better as I want.

I takes the deepest breath ye ever saw. It's that deep I could swim three lengths wi it. Underwater.

Sonny Hammil's door.

I takes a last look down before settin about it. Gal's got the arm round Septic givin the old pals stuff.

I don't boot an kick it like Gal I just flip the letterbox up an down so if Sonny Hammil catches me I'll be able to say I never kicked it an mibbi he'll just boot ma arse. He does that when he's in a good mood. He spins ye round an toes ye in the hole an lets ye go. That's alright. It's only sore for a day.

I gives it five flips sactly. **Christ!** I'm only in the cupboard an Sonny Hammil's tuggin at the squeaky door handle cursin an swearin.

I hears his boots breakin the slabs an he's shoutin down at Gal an Septic.

See anybody at ma door? By Christ I'll mudder them so I will. Mudder them.

Gal does his big primary school voice – *No Miiiiiiisteeeer Haaaamiiillll,* he goes.

There's this big pause. There's frightenin in the air. Electric silence. I can feel it. Nothin's happenin. I'm tryin to see through the cracks in the door but it's an empty bit of the lane. Sonny Hammil must've been wonderin to give Gal an Septic a doin for the sake of it. But then his crunchin boots come up the lane. They flash like lights as he goes by. STEEL-TOED. He's put his steelies on special. He never had them on the first time. Sure of it. I'm wantin to come out the cupboard but what if he sees me? Ye've got to wait till he goes back in the house an when he's tellin Betty all about it ye scoot across the garden. Pronto.

Areeeba! Areeba! Areeba! I shouts after I vaults the fence.

Sit down an don't you bother yer arse Sonny. Here's a wee cup of tea's the last thing I heard in the cupboard.

It's Septic now. He's slidin through the grass like an eel. Gal says he's that black Sonny Hammil'd probably stand on him if he came out now.

See me? I'm sidekick. See ma maw? She's sidekick too. She can tell when there's somebody goin to die or somethin bad's goin to happen. See that Bloody Sunday? In Ireland? When all these people got shot for nothin? The day before it she says somethin bad was goin to happen in Ireland. *It's goin to be a black day for the Irish,* she goes an rattle rattles at the sink. An it did. But I think I'm sidekick too. I just know Sonny Hammil's in sprintin position in the lobby wi all the locks an chains off. But instead of Alf Tupper Tough of the Track runnin shoes wi spikes he's got big boot ye right on the hole dead sore steelies on.

Septic's at the door an I'm waitin on Sonny Hammil's hand comin out an draggin him through the letter box like Roadrunner. But Septic's not waitin on that. He's smilin like First Holy Communion.

He turns an does a real fart on the door. Then what does he do? He's got his hands behind him like a ducks tail an he flips the letterbox up an down still laughin at us. But if that's not enough he back heels it. He rams his heel in an cracks the glass. All I remember's this Addams Family grin slidin in the cupboard. Sonny Hammil appears like he just sprung up out the garden.

It's me an Gal on the gatepost walk.

YAAAAAAAAAAAAAAAAAA AAAAAAAAAARHRHRHRH RHRHRHRH!!!

DID YOU DID YOU???????SEE??????? MA DOOR MA DOOR?????!?!?!?!?!?!?!

He's in the cupboard Mr Hammil, says Gal pointin. That was the plan. Ye'd think I'd laugh an laugh but I feel sick. I feel sick at three things.

1   Sonny Hammil's heavy body movin in his steel-toed boots.

2   Septic's eye glarin through a crack in the door.

3   Gal lookin pleased.

There's two reasons why Gal lookin pleased makes me sick.

1   I spected him to laugh.

2   I spected him to be scared like me.

But I've not got time to worry about all that. Sonny Hammil's breakin his nails on the cupboard. Septic's bony fingers don't last long holdin it shut. Sonny Hammil's even madder now cos his nails're bleedin. Gushin.

He lurches in an drags Septic out by the hair. There's bread goin everywhere.

There's this metal railin all round the cupboard an ye can't run sept for past the door. But that's where Sonny Hammil is. The first boot shakes the whole of Cadzow. Sonny Hammil looks at blood runnin out his nails an sets right in about him. *Watch ma asthma! Watch ma asthma!* Septic's shoutin. But asthma's the last thing Sonny Hammil's watchin. He's watchin where he's aimin his boot for the best result.

YA WEE BOOT AWCH FUCKIN BOOT AWCH BASTARD I'LL TEACH BOOT AWCH YE A LESSON YE'LL NEVER BOOT AWCH FORGET.......YE'LL NO BOOT AWCH BE CHAPPIN ANY FUCKIN BOOT AWCH CUNT'S FUCKIN BOOT AWCH DOOR BOOT AWCH AGAIN BOOT AWCH

Gal strides out the lane. I've not seen this walk on him before. It's the kind of walk a gunslinger uses when he's shot two guys down in the dust outside the saloon. BLAM! BLAM! *Bite the dust ya sons of cowpokes.*

I'm turnin back all the time. Sonny Hammil's layin in about Septic an he's curled in a ball givin out wee moans wi every kick. The whole street's out watchin now but he's not stoppin. The street starts eggin him on. *Kick his skwinty head in Sonny,* an all this they're goin. Betty's on his back tryin to pull him off but it's no use. Septic's gettin the doins owed out to the last million that chapped his door an ran away. Or screwed his van. I shivers. Could've been me. Could've been Gal.

He's gettin killed Gal!

Deserves it, c'mon, he goes, an tugs me away. To stop maself bein sick I change the subject.

What about the loaf, Gal?

Eh?

The loaf?

What about it?

What ye goin to tell yer maw?

Next thing his fancy walk stopped an he tripped over the kerb. His maw'll kill him. I starts thinkin that mibbi Septic deserves it too.

C'mon we'll check the Moorhens, is all he can say an he walks away like an escapin convict this time. Head down an straight legs. The Moorhens that's good I'm sayin in maself. I'll get one for ma da. Things isn't as bad as they look.

Krick's Chips

Guess who's in the chippy? Mackenzie. Me an Gal hide
behind this motor. He's shoutin an bawlin at Krick. Krick's
great. Everybody likes Krick. A poke of chips for runnin
round the bettin shop an stickin his line on. An two pickles.
Or beetroots. Whatever ye want. Jerkins even. Me an Gal's
got it twice. It's like gettin a Christenin piece.

These two lassies're singin 'Can the Can' but they're
watchin Mackenzie out the side of their eyes. He's goin
mental kickin the counter an Krick's wavin his arms about
an shoutin all this stuff in Tally. He always does that. He
talks in Scottish till he's mad an then it's Tally. Some people
go in an pressonate him, *Eh ah Krick ah Poke ah chipsah I'll ah
kick ah yer ah head in ah,* they go. But Krick just says, *Getah to
fuckah an noah comeah backah!*

But this day ye can see he's just about to lift the big jar of
pickles, or jerkins, or pickled eggs an dunt Mackenzie's head.
But Mackenzie's dodgin about so he can't. *That's Krick's party
trick,* Gal says. He split Big Gal's head like a kipper wi an Irn
Bru bottle this night. Tried to not pay for his fish supper.
Special an two pickles an a beetroot he thinks – he's not sure.

It was a right laugh, says Gal, *ma da sittin on the chippy floor
wi the blood runnin out his head an this big Special Fish hangin
out his mouth like a lizard's tongue till this dog ran away wi it.*
But he's a liar Gal. He wasn't there. It was his Jim. That's
what I'm on about – that's Gal usin his Jim's patter. But I

never say nothin when he's kiddin on it was him cos sometimes I tell lies an he never bothers.

The two lassies're laughin at Mackenzie now. He's comin out the door

swag   gerin

that much that his soldiers're nearly scrapin off the ground. He stares right in the lassies' eyes an opens his fish supper without lookin. I wish I could do that – stare right in lassies eyes an open ma fish supper at the same time. Gal's the same. None of us two can talk to lassies right.

We duck right down an he walks away to the left eatin his grub. All the other guys hangin about get out his road. Mackenzie's got **Come On Then** bleached out on the back of his jacket.

See if he turned round he'd see the two lassies givin him the fingers an walkin

like   him.

It'd be a laugh only me an Gal can't laugh cos he's goin to kill us. Member? I do.

He disappears an Krick's pressin against the steamy glass to see where he's went. No Mackenzie, so me an Gal stand up an Krick goes back to flickin up chips.

Close there Derrick. Mackenzie's a zoony. Gal's walkin away, the lassies're singin 'Can the Can' again an Krick's dishin up chips.

WELL! Does Mackenzie not come

zooooooooooooooooooooooooooooooooooooomin back? He runs right past the chippy crushin his fish supper an droppin it.

Everybody's amazed. Krick skweeks his nose along the glass followin Mackenzie. The whole chippy an the lassies swing their heads. Me an Gal's not botherin hidin now.

I'm wonderin what's that scary Mackenzie runs away when this Polis motor draws up. But they're not chasin Mackenzie, he thinks that's it but it's not. They're only down for chips.

This Polis gets out an just as he's chappin the windae Krick's givin him the I've got yer stuff ready right here signal. There's this guy in the back. I think it's Mulligan. He's signallin for us to open the door. But what can we do? We're only me an Gal.

The Polis is in the chippy an Krick's goin on in Tally an Scottish about Mackenzie givin him abuse. All the Polis wants is his chips so he's noddin away kiddin on he's listenin. But soon as he gets the chips its ta ta Krick an out he goes. Krick's voice bounces off all the walls when the door opens. The door swings shut an the windaes steam up an Krick's fadin away in the mist an shoutin at customers.

The Polis jumps in an speeds off wi Mulligan droolin at the smell of fish suppers. It's no fun gettin lifted. Me an Gal's been lifted. Twice. I'll tell ye after.

JESUS!!! Who comes along gruntin an puffin an pantin but the mad Boxer Dog. It snaffles Mackenzie's crushed supper an limps off wi its toe nails clickin off the slabs. It's slabbers're meltin the paper.

Big Sticks an Tarry Pits

Mackenzie went the way we were goin so we had to go away round the long way. We never wanted to go away round the long way cos we never really knew the paths an stuff. Gal figured we could get back to the Moorhens an keep the edge up for Mackenzie an all.

We can keep the edge up for Mackenzie an get to the Moorhens an all, he says.

To get to the Slaggy the way that's not the Oil Pond way ye've got to go away up the West End park an come in through the Tarry Pits. That's where the Devil lives. It's all these tarry pits an they're bubblin in the summer. Sometimes there's smoke an flames.

Don't youse go near them Tarry Pits again aul Nick'll have yees for his dinner! That was ma granny tryin to get the tar off of our Caroline's frock wi a block of Stork. But that was years ago. This time the tar sticks on our feet just. It's this thin surface an if ye go through that it's molten tar. It's like walkin on a drum skin. An if ye burst it ye fall all the way to the centre of the earth. **AS** ➜ *Journey To The Centre Of The Earth.* Me an Gal love that.

Anyway it's all changed when we get there. Don't mind all these trees. Must've grew dead fast. Next minute we're lost. Goin the wrong way. *Sun rises in the east an sets in the west,* ma da's always sayin like that's the most important thing in the world. Every time he used to take us all down the Glen wi the big pot an the spuds he'd point at the sun.

Sun rises in the east an sets in the west, he goes tracin where the sun's goin when it lands. Up behind the chapel in Bargeddie's where it sets. I thought, *Who's ever goin to need to know all about the sun risin an settin all over the place?* But this day it comes in handy. Just goes to show ye.

Gal, know how the sun rises in the east an sets in the west? Eh?

The sun. It rises in the east an sets in the west.

What're you on about now?

Ma da says...

Oh not your da again he's always sayin somethin – he starts doin ma da – he's always doin that – it's his own da he should be slaggin.

He keeps goin, *Here some more shit to tell all yer pals son – bus stops're made out of metal.* He sticks his face right in mine.

Mackenzie's about! he goes.

So I went, *I know who can do him in.*

Who – yer granny? says Gal.

No. Ma da.

Gal bursts out laughing then starts pokin punches an actin like he can't breathe. Personatin ma da.

Shut it Gal.

But he doesn't shut it. He clamps his throat wi his hand an bumps about tryin to choke hiself. He's doin ma da still.

The next time I... draw a breath... I'm goin right down... to do that Mackenzie in – right down son, he goes.

Then he falls down dead. I bends over an snorts an oinks like a pig. That opens his eyes.

Shut it Riley!

He doesn't like it. Can give it but can't take it. I starts bein drunk.

No... oshiffer... no pig in here... no... I'm great at doin his da drunk. Gal's fizzin.

I sayed shut it!!

But I keep on goin. I've got to hold ma laughin in, …*no pig here – no shur… jist ma wife! Oshiffer.*

We bought that pig! Gal says.

I starts singin a wee song, ♪*Da – Gal – the – ugly – runt –*

stole – a – pig – an – away – he – ran.

Well at least he can run. Your da's got carrier bags for lungs, says Gal.

I picks up this stick.

Gal pulls out his sling an loads it.

Dance ya dick, he goes. He means it. But I've got the stick in the air above his head before ye can say Och Maggie Macaroni Cheese.

But I covers ma balls anyway wi ma other hand.

Gal says, *Sling's faster than a stick.*

Stick's harder than a sling, I goes.

Sling's more accurate.

Stick'll smash yer skull.

Sling'll go right through it – out the other end.

After ages starin each other out Gal's elastic starts vibratin. Ma arm's shakin too – the stick's weighin me down. Gal pulls one eyebrow down.

Quits? Gal goes.

Quits! I says an laughs a wee bit so he'll know I really want to quit but not too much so he'll think I've crapped it.

I fling the stick away. whirrrrrrrrrrrrrsiiiiiiwsh it goes

through the air an he puts his sling by. Gal whips out a bag of Flyin Saucers from his pocket.

All I wanted to tell him was the sun was settin. An I know it sets over the chapel in Bargeddie like I says. But if we're walkin south towards the Slaggy the sun should be on our right. But it's not. It's behind us so we're not walkin the right way. Unless the sun's took a wee detour.

Oh I'm fed up wi this east to west stuff – I'm goin for a wee detour the day. Signed – Yours Brightly – the Sun.

So we're lost an it's only me that knows it. I'm not tryin to tell him again.

There's white dust. Gal rubs his shoe in it wi the lifted eyebrows an his bottom lip pressin his top lip up an lookin out the side of his face. That's his puzzlin look. Some's on the ground an some's on the leafs.

I shakes a white dust branch at Gal an he investigates We're Kojakin the dust without even talkin. Not a lot of pals could do that. The Silent Detectives. The Untalkables. Randall an Hopkirk quiet as death.

Gal, d'you believe in Spacemen? I half-whispers, but I'm not lookin at him: I'm lookin in between the trees. The dark.

Eh?'s all he can say.

Mercury, Venus, Mars… life on them an that? Spacemen? Your head's puggled.

We walk on a wee bit. I'm sure I can hear feetprints but I don't say nothin. Mibbi Mulligan's escaped's what I'm thinkin. Gal's in one of them moods that wants to slag me all the time. But I can't keep quiet sometimes me. Specially when I'm feart.

Trimmer says there is, I goes.

She's not allowed to say that. She's a Catholic, says Gal wi his knows everythin face on.

She's a teacher… she's been to the Grand Canyon!

You fancy her, he blows a couple of kisses at me.

No I don't, I says.

How'd'ye hang about her like a collie dug all the time then? But Gal buys her things. He bought her this Our Lady lighter at Carfin this time.

I'm not the one that bought her an Our Lady lighter at Carfin. Oh oh ye can see he's mad. Holdin it in.

No but ye made her a pop-up birthday card. I mean – so what – everybody made her cards at her birthday. Even Ben Martin done it. But Gal writes her poems.

At least I never put a poem through her letterbox!! Gal ignores me an walks on. I've got him now.

At least I never put a poem through her letterbox!! He's still walkin away.

At least I never put a poem through her letterbox!!

...but he ignores me hard as anythin. It's Vee Et Nam. We're creepin through not breakin twigs an shovin our heads through bushes first before we pour our bodies into clearins. The ground's gettin softer an softer. Quieter an quieter.

SEPTIC COMES CRASHIN OUT

THE TREES!!

JESUS CHRIST! He's got the stick I flung away. An that's not all he's got. He's got a fat lip an a black eye. There's dried blood below his nose. Me an Gal's froze.

Heth in di tupboard Mr Hammil!!!! goes Septic, so we know what the big stick's for.

He jerks forward an me an Gal jerk back.

Gimmi dem plyin thaucers!

He grabs Gal's flyin saucers but there's this noise in the trees behind him. The east. We're froze. The three of us. Ye can't tell if Septic's givin Gal the flyin saucers or takin them. Septic turns his head an me an Gal's away doin Woody the Woodpecker.

HA HA HA HAAAA HA
HA HA HA HAAAA HA
HA HA HA HAAAA HA
HA HA HA HAAAA HA
HA HA HA HAAAA HA
HA HA HA HAAAA HA
HA HA HA HAAAA HA

When Septic turns back all he probably can see is two clouds of white dust tornadoin into the deepness of the trees.

An I'll tell ye this too – it's two close shaves cos when we're runnin there's Mackenzie sneakin the other way wi his knife out. He's lookin at where Septic is. Me an Gal zoom before he can turn. Mackenzie knows there's somethin but he can't figure it out.

We're Alf Tupper an Billy Whizz me an Gal. That's what his Jim calls us. We're blastin through the trees. I'm right behind him an our legs're sact thegether. His left leg's out an so's mine. Ma leg's stretchin under where his arse is. It's the same wi his other leg. I'm lookin right in the back of his head an whizzin along.

Nothin can stop us now. Nothin. We'll get that Moorhen's if it's the last thing we do.

The Hiss of a Thousand Snakes

THUMP THUMP

We land out the trees in white powder desert dust. Beamers of light're stretchin across at all angles. Like Stalag Thirteen. But all different colours. Red, green, blue, white, yella. This big THING is in the middle of the desert. It's a UFO landin pad. Got to be. There's searchbeams an weird machines goin everywhere. An this bleep bleepin an Cybermen. But they're not silver – they're all white like the dust I'm goin on about.

Me an Gal freeze. We've got no UFO plans.

I looks at Gal.

Gal looks at me.

There's this noise in the trees behind us.

We look at the noise.

We look back at each other.

Mackenzie! We transmit the sact same time.

We look at the UFO landin pad.

Gal does his commando *C'mon move out,* an we move into the clouds an blindin lights turnin slow an deliberate, like it's only us they're lookin for. Specimens.

Weird. Machines like I've never seen before. Not even on the telly. I don't know if Gal's never seen them before but he's walkin sact same as me so I suppose it's machines he never seen before too. Even on the telly.

Cybermen're everywhere but they haven't seen us. Next thing there's this big hiss like a thousand snakes. Like lorries when they stop – or buses. Only bigger. Gal crouches. A Cyberman materialises like *Star Trek* in this light beam. It's right in front of us. This other Cyberman holds this ray-gun thing an he's firin it.

Hchiisssssss, it's goin an this invisible ray blasts big lumps out the Cyberman that's just beamed down. He's turnin into the white dust. The spinnin lights light up its whirlwinds. He's gettin powdered man! Dusted in the hiss of a thousand snakes machine. Gal's fingers're diggin in me.

The light goes out. That's him dead.

Ohhhhmnmamna, I says to Gal an even if it's not a word Gal knew sactly – too terryfied to talk.

The hiss of a thousand snakes machine goes back on an another Cyberman beams down. He starts gettin dusted an powdered too. It's horrible. I want to throw a rock an save him. I turns round an scratches about in the dust for somethin to fling. That's when I seen Septic sniffin about the edge of the trees.

I nudges Gal.

Sep-tic, I says wi ma mouth but not wi noise.

Septic's like a bent kirby grip followin our feetprints in the dust. He's still got the stick.

There's three things frightenin me an Gal now.

1   Septic an his stick. (A wee bit.)

2   The Cyberman might see Septic an follow him right to us.

3   We can't go forward cos the death duster's there.

But Gal's offski. He's great when it's like this Gal. Any time we're dead for sure he pulls somethin out the hat! Last minute Gal he should be called. Last second.

See all that stuff I was sayin about Gal there the now? Forget it. Eejit's took us up a dead end. When I gets there he's runnin back down it at me. Trapped between Septic an a brick wall.

CYBERMEN LOAD

CYBERMAN TAKE   *AIM*

CYBERMEN TREMBLE TREMBLE *FIRE*

That's me an Gal doin the tremble tremble. I'm thinkin that's what's about to happen when who comes in the alley but Septic.

But he's not that daft Gal. When we ran in the alley we got up on these boards that run round the side of the UFO landin Pad. Septic thinks we're hidin where our feetprints stop. There's a big metal box there. He crouches sniggerin. Waitin. Ye can see his stick waverin about if ye look hard.

I picks up this gigantic rock an flings it. It stoved his head right in an the blood an brains're runnin out all over the dust.

Only kiddin.

We're crawlin along the wall like backwards spiders. Same way as the Echo only the other way round. It's that dark in the alley nobody could see us. Not even aul Nick if he escaped from the Tarry Pits. Skweek – an this chink of light's on the wall. Like magic.

Psssst! says Gal an points.

I let him think he found it. He likes to find the things first Gal. Sometimes I wait years waitin on him findin what I already found hours ago.

The chink of light's on the other side. We sneak across inches from Septic. He's talkin to hiself. An laughin. He keeps on movin his grip about the stick. Pressin his fingers tight an slackenin them again. Like he's playin rounders waitin for somebody to fling the ball.

In the cupboard Mr Hammil, he's sayin. *In the fuckin cupboard Mr Hammil,* an clenchin the stick tighter an doin this mad snigger.

We move towards the light wi our soldiers goin up an down. For a minute I thought it was just this thin line of light like ye always see on UFOs. But it's a door when we come to it.

But I still gets a fright. The aliens've got their sign painted

on it. It's a red hand an they've wrote their slogan

in Scottish under it.

NO SURRENDER

Means fight to the death. Aliens rule. Probably.

Sometimes Gal makes yer hair stand up. An not just jumpin off the Pipe into trees an all that stuff. What he does this time that makes ma hair tickle ma neck is – he puts his hand an all his fingers on the hand an the door. Next minute the door swings open an bump bump bumps off the wall.

Septic'll see the light so we jump in right away an shut the door. Last thing I sees is Septic chippin stones at the metal box. He's tryin to get the Cybermen over where he thinks me an Gal is. Just like we done to him wi Sonny Hammil. What a dick.

Inside's this big massive red hand's takin up the whole wall nearly. It smells oily an dusty. There's a row of tables an chairs an all these piece boxes lyin about. Christ! They're

even drinkin Irn Bru an Strike Cola!! Some
Aliens!!

It's scary. There's a Christopher Cushion cut ye in half
saw. Massive. Could do me an Gal same time. Gal pings one
of the teeth an sticks his tongue out.

There's a noose hangin out the roof.

This must be the courtroom, I whispers.

How?

I points at the noose an Gal swivels his eyes to drawins on
the wall. A pyramid wi a big eye in it's followin us about.
Watchin. Like our Sacred Heart Of Jesus. An right there an
then I want ma da. I don't tell Gal I want ma da but I do. Ma
maw's singin bum'd be better than this.

Mibbi the pyramid's their planet an they draw it on the
wall so they feel at home. Ma granny's got all these paintins
of Donny Gol. Mibbi they've got a maw that slaps ye for bein
down the Milky Way an a da that sits an reads the *Daily
Spaceman* wi big webbed hands stickin out? Mibbi they'd
rather be there than away down here on this stinkin wee
planet?

Next thing Gal's stopped wi his mouth hangin open. He
tugs ma eyes round his back wi his eyes. Somethin's got him.
He can't move. I leans over till I can see what it is. I'm great
at leanin over me.

I screams!! an pulls Gal. It's hands. We falls on the
floor screamin quiet. But they're not hands. They're these
rubber gloves an they're goin up an down wi this hissin
noise the same as the noise in the *Beam me up an powder me
away to nothin station.* Scottie.

UP

hisssssssssssssssssssssssssssssssssssssssss

an down

UP

hisssssssssssssssssssssssssssssssssssssssss

an down
that's what they're doin.

We're doin *what'll we do* faces. This toilet flushes. Spacemen goin to the bog!!?? Weird. Don't do it in the Pictures. Whoever heard of Superman goin – *Hold on world I'll need to go for a wee pee before I save yees...?*

We dives under a table. We're just at the diggin nails an screwin up our faces stage when the bog door opens. These giant feet come clump clumpin across the floor. I'd rather be in Sonny Hammil's cupboard now. Gal's the same. He never sayed it. He never sayed,

Oh Derrick, now that I come to think of it – I'd much rather be in good aul Sonny Hammil's cupboard – how's about you old bean what?

Can ye magine it? Anyway, this Spaceman's breathin like his nose is blocked an his teeth're glued thegether.

He clumps right to the table. Me an Gal's mouths're wide so our breaths won't make noise. Mind Hammil's steelies? Spacemen's boots're all steel – an this other black metal. An another thing – he's got steel-toed kneepads on. Like he knees ye till ye're on the deck an then cracks yer ribs wi the metal boots.

Mind I sayed I was sidekick? Well there's this piece box on the floor. I thinks, Oh oh this is the Spaceman's box.

I'm right!

He reaches this big Griller arm into the box an pulls out this thing like a chicken leg only times ten. His breath smells like diesel mixed wi lemon curd. Stinkin. Boufin. It's roastin an all. Near burns ma soldier. I thinks he's seen us so I give Gal a *I think he seen us* face. That's pullin yer mouth wide an just showin yer top teeth an noddin dead wee an quick millions of times. But Gal gives me the *No he's not seen us* look. That's stickin yer lips out like ye're about to kiss yer auntie Sadie an puttin the quiet finger on it an noddin side to side a lot slower than me. Noddy an Noddy's pal – that's us two under the table.

The big cut ye in half saw. He's started it up. I can see his hands under the edge of the table rippin through the giant bird's leg. It'll be the leg off some big pecker bird from his planet. There's blood an bits of stringy stuff comin out an all these flaps of fatty skin whirlin round on the blade an splatterin across the roof.

I still can't see his face.

Gal leans for a look. *Gulphphphp,* he goes holdin his lips thegether wi the tips of his fingers.

That's when I sees the Spaceman's face. He turns the saw off an spins round bitin right through the leg in a oner. An he's lookin right at me. His eyes're sayin – this is how I'm goin to eat you in a wee minute when I've scoffed a couple of lumps of this pecker bird.

Squeek, I goes.

Gal tries to lean again to see what I'm skweekin about.

KERRRASH

the table's in the air an there's us two wi our arms up like wee mouses scratchin their whiskers.

He's laughin an dribblin down the big lump of meat stuck in his mouth. His hairy nostrils're goin in an out. Like them plants from Venus that eat insects.

Next thing we're off the ground.

Me in one hand   an Gal in the other.

Like scales. He spits the bone away.
Ke-lunk, says the bone off the wall.

GI-ULP, says me an Gal.

He's got a red hand tattooed on his arm. 'No Surrender' under it. Yup. An alien. Definitely. Or mibbi an alien helper cos he just looks like a mad man out the Woodside Bar. I'm ready for, *Take me to your leader earthling.*

He looks at me. I'm wonderin who ma leader is.

He looks at Gal.

He looks at me again.

School d'ye go to? he says.

I don't know if it's cos he's speakin Scottish or cos of the daft question but I laugh. Well smile really. He presses his face right into mine. I can smell Buckie an his gristles're scrabin the face off me.

School? he goes again.

C C C C Columba – C C Columba High.

He seemed pleased wi that answer cos he lowers me down an pulls Gal up to near where ma face was a minute ago. I sees the peekin pyramid on his other arm. Yup. Alien for sure.

School? he goes to Gal.

Gal looks over like I know the answer an he doesn't. I mean the guy might be askin for square roots of this that an the next thing.

What's the square root of fifteen zillion Riley? says Johnny Humph.

Twenty-one an a half sir?

Twenty-one and a half what – BANANAS?

No sir – Camels.

Ouuuut HERE BOY!

But these're easy questions. That's why I'm puzzled when Gal gets it wrong.

Kirk-Kirk-shaws. Kirkshaws primary.

He's pleadin for mercy wi his eyes like a holy picture. I hate when he's like that. I'd rather he stuck the napper on the guy even if he is goin to kill the two of us.

He lets Gal go decidin to believe him or not.

I'm nearly greetin. Somethin's tellin me Gal's tellin lies so as to get away an he's goin to leave me an an an...

No he doesn't. No he doesn't Mister. He goes to ma school, I blurts it out. I felt bad about it. Gal looks like he can't believe I sayed it. But he's good Gal – he never mentioned it again. He could've made me look like a dick in front of the whole school. But he never. That's pals for ye. That's me an Gal all over the back.

The Spaceman grabs Gal an gives him the gristly chin treatment. *Name?* He goes.

Stephen Patrick....

Now there's a name he never liked. He throws the two of us in the corner without askin me mine. I'm thinkin I've got a good name even if I've not got a good school an that might get us off. But no. We're slung in the corner an he's givin us the beady eye. It's only when he turns away I see two peekin pyramids tattooed on the back of his baldy head. I can't move. They're worse than his front eyes. *Right I'll show ye what happens to wee Fenian thieves!* He goes, an starts the saw.

It's that Fenian word again. Gal's da says they can tell the way ye walk an talk. It still puzzles me how people can tell ye're a Fenian from the way ye walk an the way ye talk. Christ I never even knew I was one till I asked ma da thon time ages ago. Gal's one too. It's good we're the same wi that an all. Except when we meet Aliens that don't like Fenians. He starts walkin towards us again wi that look that means he's got a million sore tortures for us.

This   amazin

RRRRRRRRRRRR RRRRRRAAAAAAA AAAAAAAAAAA AAACKET

fills the room cos the bold Gal's flung a handful of nails on the saw. Six inchers. They're pingin an shoomin all over the place like a war. There's holes appearin in the windaes an the walls. Me an Gal's lucky to be alive the day. Tellin ye! Four eyes is all over the place an me an Gal bolt in the alley.

Should've seen Septic's face when we bolt past him. Right out the alley. Flyin. He curves his body round an looks in the metal box. All these Cybermen start chasin us. We jook left through the white dust desert. I sees Septic sneakin in the bothy. But it's not a UFO landin pad. I thought that's what it was. It makes Itchycooblue. The same signs that were on the sheets Gal spotted over the Slaggy're all over the outside of the buildins. The stuff ma da worked wi. The stuff that gave him Bestos.

We're tryin to run through the sand-dunes. But we can only get the run ye use in the dream ye're tryin to get away from the ghost. Like ye're runnin through heavy treacle.

From the right this JCB shovel comes out the sand liftin the ground sendin us sideways. Sand's waterfallin from the shovel lut up a horrible orange by the spinnin lights.

From the front a fork lift's blindin us wi white light.

When we swerve left this massive bulldozer shovel tries to bulldoze us. I swear I heard laughin comin out the shovel.

We turn back but crowds of men're right on us an growlin an pointin. One of their fingers brushes ma arm.

Zipidee doo da – round the edge of the bulldozer an down a big sand hill an up this other one. The men're all laughin an pointin like we're runnin into a pond of crocodiles.

KERASH an we're right through piles of Itchycooblue sheets. KERASH KERASH KERASH KERASH an we're at the trees in no time.

POP

POP

we're off usin our different ways plan.

I can't go on till I tell ye what happened to Septic. Gal – his Jim heard it off Plook Murphy. Septic's cousin.

Septic's sittin in the place me an Gal got chased out. He's dippin Yo Yo's in a cup of soup. He's sittin there, says Jim, wi his hands wrapped round the cup keepin warm.

Big baldy Alien appears in the doorway.

Septic gives it his stupit teethless grin an he's flashin the skwint all over the place for an escape route. There's none.

The guy comes in an starts the saw. He cut Septic's fingers off. Then...

But he stopped. Never sayed what happened next. Not for our ears he says. We gave him two bob so as he'd mibbi tell us.

Gimmi all yer dosh an mibbi I'll tell yees.

He never.

Smile for Mackenzie

I'm goin faster an faster through the trees.

Faster an faster. *I'm a car I'm a plane I'm a fast fast jet,* I'm sayin over an over,

I'm a car I'm a plane I'm a fast fast jet, I'm a car I'm a plane I'm a fast fast jet, I'm a car I'm a plane I'm a fast fast jet, I'm a car I'm a plane I'm a fast fast jet, I'm a car I'm a plane I'm a fast fast jet, I'm a car I'm a plane I'm a fast fast jet, I'm a car I'm a plane I'm a fast fast jet, I'm a car I'm a plane I'm a fast fast jet, I'm a car I'm a plane I'm a fast fast jet.

The moon's in the sky. Full.

I crash into this clearin an who whips round like he's been pullin his puddin but mad SAS Mackenzie. The knicker section's pinned to a tree. An somethin else too. There's somethin shinin on the tree. Wrigglin. Yup definitely somethin wrigglin. I don't see it right cos I'm spinnin on one heel tryin to grab maself back into the trees again. I've got a branch.

Smile for Mackenzie! says Mackenzie.

But I'm already pullin maself back in the forest. I'm about to let rip wi a Woody the Woodpecker. Mibbi chuck a couple of rocks back over ma soldiers, when,

Gal thumps into me at full tilt comin out the trees.

We're a pile of washin an Mackenzie gets Gal an pulls him up to his face. Hard men always do that – pull ye up to their face to frighten ye.

As Mackenzie breathes on him I sneaks the sling out Gal's back pocket an chuck it. Member the ball-bearin?

Mackenzie starts punchin Gal on the side of the head. DING DING DONG. Even I can feel it. Blue flashes like train wires at night're comin out Gal's ears. His head's bouncin about like he's made out of rags but he doesn't even scream. He's used to doins is Gal. His brothers an sometimes his da when he's drunk. An his maw! His maw? She lays in about him wi the brush. Not the big floor brush. No way. That's too hard to swing. She lays in about him wi the wee stair brush. *Ye could kill a horse wi that,* ma da says. *Kill a horse.*

But he's not Superman Gal so he starts whimperin. Not roarin an greetin like you an me. Just a wee whimper. Mackenzie swings him into this tree stump wi a hell of a thud. I fling the last of the flyin saucers over ma soldier.

ZZZZZIIIIIIIINGNGNG

Mackenzie scuds me a Enter The Dragon on the head. *Ha ooow eee,* he goes, jerkin his head like he's got a sore neck. Down I goes. I rolls in a ball. Gal's a ball too. That was one of our plans – if ye're gettin a hell of a doin ye roll in a ball till ye can uncoil an run.

When he's layin into Gal I notice the somethin on the tree again. It's a frog. An shinin below it – stuck in the tree – is Mackenzie's big blade. The frog's pinned to the tree wi thorns. Feet an arms. Crucified. But it's still not givin in. I'd've gave in if I was nailed through the hands an the feet to a tree. But this frog's shovin its white belly in an out an pullin an tuggin. One of its flippers rips free. There's blood runnin down its green arm an across its white belly. Then this other thud goes into me an I can't see the frog no more.

Columba came in ma head. I wanted to go to Gal,
Remember Columba Gal? but he was doin roll in a ball.

All these pictures're goin through ma head. Dead animals
pinned to the blackboards an splattered over walls.
Hamsters, goldfish, rabbits, an all sorts chopped in bits.
Mouses flattened into books.

But Mackenzie pulls ma head back like cowboy films.
He's an Indian an I'm wounded an he's on ma back sittin.
He's got ma head back an he's got the knife at ma neck goin
to cut ma throat. I'm thinkin of Gal's da's pig an it's neck
sliced like a purse. I can't get it out ma head.

Gal's greetin.

Mackenzie presses the knife harder so he's got his other
hand free. He gets somethin out his pocket. It's a tin of
lighter petrol. The same yella tins he uses to set fire to nests
wi yunks in them.

Gal's lookin out the corner of his eye. Mackenzie squirts it
all over the ground like the can's peein. Over next to Gal an
then in wavy lines back to ma hands. He covers ma hands an
arms an squirts it in ma hair. Ye'd think the first thing ye'd
think is how terryfyin it is. But see the first thing I thinks?
The first thing I thinks is how cold it is. I feel it runnin in cold
rivers over ma skull. It's like the stuff yer maw puts on ye
when ye've got nits. I starts thinkin about Brown letters.

In the Primary the Nurse comes. The whole school gets
looked at. If ye've got Nits ye get a Brown letter. Gal was a
year below me at St James's. This time the Nurse came an I
got a Brown letter. Ma maw got them out wi the loashun an
that wee Derbac comb that rips the hair out yer head. But I'm
fly. I sticks the Brown letter up ma jook. It's playtime an
we're all out in the yard. Nobody else's got a Brown letter.
Gal's the other side of the yard. He shouts an runs over. He
looks worried.

Guess what? he goes.
What?
Guess what happened to me?

What?

He pulls a Brown letter out. John Gerard Price starts shoutin.

Gal got a Brown letter!! Look everybody – Gal got a Brown letter.

The yard's The Day The World Stood Still for a minute. Next thing it's dancin round Gal an singin. Gal's in the middle wi his head down an the letter's on the ground. Every time he kicks it away they fling it back in his face.

♪Gallacher, Gallacher, spots on yer bum an beasts in yer hair,

they're singin. An they're pointin at him so he's the middle of a big wheel. The ones that don't point's holdin their bellies. I think they're laughin but all the sound's mixed thegether like voice soup. He's lookin at me. I just walked away an left him in the heavin sea. He never mentioned it. Not a word. I walked away pressin the letter against ma jumper wi ma belly. Must've looked like I needed the toilet.

But it's petrol. It's petrol I smell now. He lights this lighter. I can see the flame shimmerin in Gal's eyes an flickin across his face.

Next minute I feel Mackenzie leanin over an there's whooshin flames zig zaggin an the lickin light of fire's comin at me. But that's not all. He lights the lighter in front of ma face. Whizzes it past ma fringe a couple of times an his laughin's echoin across the Slaggy. In the gaps in the flames I can see how dark it's got. It's night. Pitch.

Next thing Mackenzie's up an laughin. Gal's slappin ma head like ding dong bells. It's on fire. Ma head's on fire.

Ma head's on fire?

Ma head's on fire! I screams.

Ma head's on fire!

Gal whips his sloppy joe over ma head an rubs like ma maw dryin ma hair. It's black dark an singed hair an petrol an smoke an Mackenzie's laugh pourin up the sleeves an in the neck. Gal's slaps're givin it the bells of St Martin's. ♪*You owe me five farthins,* is goin round an round in me an ♪*When will you pay me?* an thud I'm on the deck an it's black. Black an quiet.

When I wake up it's Gal dabblin water on ma head. It's like a Christenin. He's pourin water over ma forehead out an aul shoe. Ma head's on his lap. Then he's dippin a lump of moss in the shoe an wipin ma head. Stars're comin out.

Thought ye were a gonner there Derrick, he goes.

I grunts. I could've talked but I just grunted.

Lucky it's just yer hair.

I feels ma face. Nothin melted. I'm sad an glad it's just ma hair.

If it was ma face I'd be able to get a great story all about it. Joanne Brennan'd wonder what happened.

I remember the frog. I look up. Gal looks up too. Next thing the two of us is at the tree. I'm recovered sept for frazzled hair. The frog's dead. There's a big stab wound in its side an it's covered in petrol. But he never burnt it. Gal's thinkin Columba same as me. I know he's thinkin Columba same as me cos his face is straight like it isn't tryin to say anythin. But his eyes're wide. A special wide. They're not wide at the top they're only wide at the bottom. Like he's stretched the bottom of his eyes.

Mackenzie! he goes.

He didn't mean Mackenzie pinned the frog to the tree. We knew that. He meant Mackenzie done all that horrible stuff in Columba.

I need to tell ye what happened in Columba. That's the school I'm at now. Gal's there too. 1M4. I'm 2K4.

Psychos Volcanoes an Megaphones

When I was in first year me an Gal played up the Street sometimes.

Used to doss about all the aul buildins or look in the canal for sticklebacks. The canal's flat an black. It's deep an fulla dead bodies. *There's that many drunk people fell in ye could get drunk drinkin it,* ma granda used to say.

I'm tellin ye so ye can see what Mackenzie's really like. So ye know me an Gal's not makin him out worser. Everybody used to wonder who done that in Columba. Ye were always spicious of everybody. There was a time everybody all thought me an Gal done it. Even the Polis.

We're up the Street behind the Circle bar doin nothin. There's these dungeons an we're in them smashin empty wine bottles till this aul tramp from the Model chased us. *I'm the Devil,* he shouts, an chases us. *Bells an bubbles.*

So we're watchin this drip of water comin down from the gutterin away up the size of two houses an a bus stop. Tenements they called them but nobody lived there any more. It was only the Circle an this other shop an Yogi's Bar. Better than yer average bar's what is sayed under the name.

Me an Gal liked that. Yogi played for Celtic when they won the European Cup that Gal looks like.

The houses still had curtains an they were flappin out the broke glass every time pigeons shot out or flew back in. There was millions of pigeons. Millions. There was that many pigeons at the Fountain in them days ye thought it was night if they flew over.

Gal stares up. Miles. It makes me dizzy. Sick. There's four floors. The one on the ground an the one above's all bricked up.

That's so's ye can't break in the pubs, says Gal.

On the two top floors there's no bricks. But they're eerie. Spooky. Like somebody's watchin. Wi the wavin curtains it's like the people that lived there had to leave in a hurry.

Gal's got a plan. I hate it when he's got a plan. He starts shinnin up the drainpipe. I'm talkin a rusty aul pipe that looks like only the muck's holdin it on the wall.

C'mon! he goes, swingin his head over his soldiers an laughin. For a minute he's like one of them wooden dolls out a Horror Film.

I starts climbin. The pipe's that wide I can hardly hold on. It's wide as a team ball. Gal knows what I'm thinkin.

It gets thinner up here.

Ma knuckles're scrapin off the wall. Bleedin. Every floor there's another pipe that comes off the one that goes straight up. It goes out to the left at an angle under the windaes. Gal's balancin on the third one up. Facin me! I reaches the second an ma cheek's face to face wi the wall.

Don't look down, he shouts.

I looks down an it's all

I nearly broke the pipe skweezin it.

Gal scoots up the next floor. A step an a skip an he's in a windae. I'm too scared to go down now. Ma head's sayin there's another way out the buildin once ye're in. Must be. I inches up the pipe. Bit by bit. Gal's lowerin this curtain for me. No way I'm lettin go. Not a hope. I gets where the pipe goes out like a tree branch under the windaes. Gal's stretchin but he can't reach me.

This is the worst bit. Ye've got to walk yer feet onto the bit of pipe that goes under the windaes. When yer feet're in the middle ye've to shove off the straight up pipe an tilt over an grab the windae sill.

What ye doin up there? The Devil Tramp shouts. Gal flings some chair legs at him an shouts, *Fuck off ya aul dosser.*

The fright makes me shove off. I'm on ma way up for ages. I'm balanced for more ages. Not holdin nothin. Then it's ages again an I grabs the flappin curtain an Gal grabs me.

If I let you go ye're a gonner, he goes.

Don't don't Gal. Get me in. Get me in, I says. Too right!

We're in the dusty quiet of the buildins an the Devil Tramp's voice is shoutin up the walls over the roof. Like he's miles away in a forest. *I'm The Devil – Prince of Darkness – Lord of Evil,* an all stuff like that he's goin.

The close stairs look like the deepest woolly carpet ye ever seen. But it's white. A gigantic weddin cake. No a frozen waterfall – that's it. Gal jumps off the windae ledge an lands on it. Kerrrrrrrrrrrunch. It's pigeon shite. Millions. Like smelly icin. *Coo coo pooory coo* the pigeons're goin. They're everywhere.

They've not seen anybody in here for years probably. We starts goin down the stairs like Neil Armstrong an Buzz Aldrin. Big daft steps we're takin an crunchin in to our ankles. It's slobbery when ye break the surface. Smells like burnt matches. Next thing we're on this landin. Three doors. Kelly Duffy an McBride. I always remember stupit wee things like door names. We goes in Kelly's.

Our tongues're cats tongues on the roofs of our mouths. I try sloshin up some grog but it's no use. Ma mouth's like Dundyvan floor. The light's comin in the front windaes an landin on the shite-icin in big horror-film squares. We sneak over an peek out the side so nobody'll see us down in the Street.

They look that funny down there. Wee wimmin's shoppin bags tiltin them over every time they put a furry boot forward. Brown penguins.

Brown Penguins Gal. Look!
That's ma granny.
Your granny's been dead for years.
Ma other granny.
Is it?
No. It's your maw. Oh wait a minute your maw's a lot fatter than that. More like a Polar Bear.

Then he starts walkin about blowin his cheeks out an stampin big holes in the shite-icin.

This is her walkin down the pavement an breakin all the slabs.

I stare out the windae. There's men stridin away up the pub. An gangs up closes wi their head's thegether over somethin. Shopliftin probably. Jimmy the Hoover's there. *Best shoplifter in the Brig,* Gal says. He just hoovers stuff up his sleeve. I like lookin an nobody knowin. Great. Gal's back lookin too. I smiles at him. He thinks it's great too.

We get a laugh at the aul papers that's everywhere. Nineteen canteen. Then we're fed up.

McBride's was the place alright. We pressed the door open enough to squeeze in. It's the icin that's stoppin us. We go in. Gal then me. There's this other door wi glass an we pressed that open. Soon as we opened it all these wings're flappin like heaven. Like a trillion angels appeared over our heads. I trips over Gal pullin at the door tryin to get out.

The pigeons rush over us like a river. There's ones that can't fly runnin up ma back an slappin off ma cheeks. **Whoosh** an **Whoosh** they're goin. There's no end. This big wrigglin ribbon of white an grey's waterfallin round the glass door an rushin out the gap we left in the front.

I can magine them explodin out onto the backs where the Devil Tramp was. It's bats he'll think they are. Devil bats. Vampires.

There's this pigeon takin runs an bumpin off a windae. There's a wee hole at the bottom of the glass. A pigeon comin back in changes it's mind when it sees us. It's funny. It falls backwards off the windae ledge. The last thing I see is its wee lumpy feet.

Ye want to have seen it when the dust settled. Couldn't get a better room for two egg collectors. There's millions of wee volcanoes. There's mibbi one volcano an then another volcano growin out that an two growin out that an on an on. The room's covered. Wee volcanoes covered in snow only the rim's grey like the heat's melted the snow.

I'm waitin for smoke when Gal knows what they are. I was just about to know what they were. I was at that bit where ye think somethin's somethin else an there's a wee minute before ye know what it really is. Yer brain knows but yer mouth can't shout it yet. That'll be what ma da means about openin ma mouth wi ma head not in gear.

Nests!!!! says Gal, crunchin into the middle of them. But he crushes eggs on the way. An that's bad luck.

That's bad luck that Gal so it is.

What?

Standin on eggs.

He looks down. Yella an red's runnin down a volcano like lava. Like miniature Hell's exploded an the guts of wee demons got spurtled up. I'm waitin on Aul Nick pokin his head up an sayin, *What the Hell's this then?*

He looks over all guilty.

Bad luck's all I can say.

He ignores me. I think he felt bad. He starts only standin on volcanoes wi no eggs. I makes ma way over in his feetprints so I don't kill any yunks not born yet. There's more eggs than I ever seen in the one wee bit in all ma life. More than ASDA.

Gal starts collectin. Pigeons're alright. Better than a Blackie's but not as good as a Crow's or a Chaffinch or somethin. But a million pigeon's eggs? Well! Swaperama that's what we'll be havin I'm thinkin.

We're collectin them in our jumpers. They're rollin about heavy an clickin off each other. Me an Gal's these two smiles crunchin about the surface of Mars. Sometimes a bold pigeon flaps in an buzzes us. But we're only takin one out a nest an only if it's not cloakin. We're quiet like a bank robbery. Safety deposit boxes. Diamonds. Ye've got to hold the eggs up to the light to see if there's any red. Gal's the best at that. If I'm not sure he x-rays it.

Sh! goes Gal.

Eh?

Shh, d'ye hear that?

I listens. It's cars outside an a train on the bridge an people walkin about the Street an this megaphone about votin.

The megaphone goes again.

...out ...cover everything ...chance ...last chance

That! goes Gal scared.

I'm wonderin what he's scared of a votin megaphone for.

It's the Polis! he goes,

Ma head changes from a votin megaphone to a Polis megaphone an the blood drains out me an I starts shakin. The shite-icin's suckin me in. I can't move ma feet.

SLAP

Gal slaps me. I can move ma feet now. We stick the eggs back in any aul nest. They won't know what's what when they crack out. Like that stuff about knowin yer maw but not knowin yer da ma maw goes on about.

We run down the stairs into damp coldness. It's pitch black. We feel about. It's all bricked up like a grave.

If you don't come out we'll send the dogs in, shouts the megaphone like a Scottish Dalek.

Woof woof, go the dogs in case we think they're kiddin.

We run about like rats but there's no way out. It's a maze. The pigeons're comin back by the barra load. It's like runnin through bats in a Dracula film or *The Birds.* Hitchcock. I'm greetin. But Gal was greetin too an so would you be.

What'll we do Gal? What'll we do?

Gal turns his hands up.

Come down or the dogs go in, says the Dalek.

Woof GRRRRRR woof, says the dogs.

We'll have to give ourselfs up, Gal goes.

I bursts out greetin.

What else can we do? goes Gal, holdin ma soldiers lookin straight in ma eyes. I nods like I agree wi him. But I'm greetin cos I never wanted to go back down that pipe.

Me an Gal peek out the back. There's Polis cars an Polis men an wimmin an people passin that's stopped. They're all lookin up. The whole town.

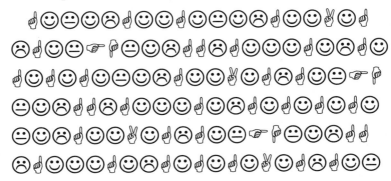

The whole town's out there, says Gal. *Ma maw'll kill me.*

The Polis started laughin when they seen us. The one wi the big alsatians took them away. Even the dogs were grinnin an noddin their heads.

Oh ho – another wasted day there Rover!

Too right Rex. Too right!

Right boys come down this instant, says the megaphone. But it's not doin a Big Polis Dalek voice this time. It's doin a Teacher Dalek voice. Like it's fed up an wants to go home. There's electric laughin at the end of his sentences.

We'll be the laughin stock, says Gal greetin. *Ma maw hates the laughin stock worse than anythin.*

It's the first I heard Gal sayin laughin stock. Mibbi that's how ye grow up. Ye start usin their words. Before ye know it all yer words're what yer maw an da say. An that's you. Big.

Gal starts climbin down first. They're chippin stones at his arse the Polis. An clappin when it's a good shot. Then it's me. I'm perched on the tree branch pipe an still holdin the windae. I can't let go. The pipe's vibratin.

Come down, the Polis're shoutin. They're not chippin stones at me. I'm probably not as good a target as Gal. Movin target him the way he scooted down.

MOVE! shouts this big fat voice.

But I can't let go. I need to let go an grind ma face along the wall an catch the straight up pipe. But ma hands're takin orders from nobody.

People're laughin up. The sky's spinnin an birds're attackin me. I feels dizzy again. Pigeons're peckin ma knuckles. I'm about to fall when Gal shouts up.

Alf Tupper Tough of the AWWWCH!!!, a big Polis slaps him, *Shut it you. You're in enough trouble as it is!* he goes, an hits him some more ding dong dunts.

I let go an tilts over. I know you think it's nothin – him shoutin *Alf Tupper* an me lettin go an catchin the pipe. But this surge went through me an I felt good. I felt great bein Gal's pal even if the Polis had us for sure.

So. I gets down an the crowd clap an cheer like we're Celtic. Gal gets a cuff on the head for shoutin *IRA*. That's his brothers that teach him that. It's the Irish Publican Army. Gal's brothers paint it on the walls. An FKB. They paint that too. I don't know what that is. Gal say's it's fuckin krazy bastards.

We get took up the Polis Station.

KELLLANG

They locked us in this cell.

We'd never been locked up before. We start fidgetin an gettin bored. But it's not easy to keep me an Gal bored. No sir. Not even in a Polis Cell. We starts this game wi what's wrote on the door.

DAMAGE WILL RESULT IN PROSECUTION. That's what's wrote in big red letters. All these other names of mental people an gang names're scraped in the walls. Some of the names I seen on the Pipe're in there. **SCON.** JAMEPA. BIGGLES. **BOON.** DOODS. **BANGLADESH.** GAL. DAIZ. **Y-KIRK.** BONZO. **DYKES.** RIO. SHOLTZ. **CADZOW BOOT BOYS.** ROCKABILLY DILLY. **RIO.** J HOOVER. MILKY BAR. **RADAR.** KERZO. **SHAWS. EDDIE THE DUCK.** LANG L TOI. PAT THE LEG. S. TOI. JB. CLOORY. BIMBO. PILKY. **TAMLA HILL.** DOC. VINNY. **VAMBO. DIZZY DES DEE.** BAR-G. **DAVY DOOM.** K GEE. **PIRATES.**

Damage will result in prosecution, says Gal.
I goes, *Prosecution will result in damage.*
Result will damage in prosecution.
Will damage result in prosecution?
Will prosecution result in damage?
It's me, *Will result in prosecution damage?*
In damage will prosecution result?
In prosecution will damage result?
In result will prosecution damage. Good yin Gal.
In damage prosecution will result
In prosecution damage will result.
In result prosecution will damage.
Em em em, Gal's goin when we hear this noise.

CLICK PLOD CLICK PLOC CLICK PLOD

RATTLE RATTLE

THE DOOR SWINGS OPEN

An in walks this BIG POLIS. He stands an stares an then goes, *Right youse two.*

He grabs us by the scruff along this corridor stinkin of disinfectant an flings us in wi three Polis. An a CID Gal says it was.

That's a CID, he whispers. *No uniform.*

It's him that talks, the CID. The rest're drinkin tea an smokin.

What's this then? he says, an flings crumpled paper on the desk. He looks at us.

Who's Derrick Riley?

I'm just about to say me when Gal nods.

The CID bangs ma head off the table. Not sore – just so it'll make a noise.

What are you doing wi a map of Columba School?

I twists ma head an squints at him. This Polis folds the paper out an that's what it is right enough – a map of Columba. Ma name's wrote at the bottom.

Well son? CID shouts. Gal's gettin glad he had no map.

Well? He goes an **bangs** ma head three times.

Sore.

AWWCH!! Can't member.

He starts sayin we screwed Columba two nights ago an pinned the hamsters to the blackboard. An stabbed darts through the goldfishes' eyes an squashed mouses in biology books an wrote stuff on the wall wi hamster blood.

We denied it an denied it. I could hardly see through ma cryin. Gal even tried to tell them about how we never take cloakin eggs even. But then they started goin on about how we were breakin into Yogi's.

I sayed, *That's a bit daft when it was open,* an got a SALAP in the kisser. It took them ages to see we were a pair of twadgers just. Idiots the two of us. They even separated us an busted in the room an sayed Gal was makin alligators about me. Be as well tellin me Albion Rovers beat Celtic.

It was only after them findin out I went to Columba they let us go. Me an Gal were terryfied for ages in case our maws an das found out. They never.

So that's that story. I was in first year. But now cos I seen the frog crucified on the tree I know who done it. Mackenzie. He's a sicko. Mad! Mental! Psycho!

The Last of the Sun

We un-crucify the frog an chuck it in a ditch. Its white belly's just under the water's black mirror. The moon's reflected in broke lines on the rippled circles. Soon the moon's still – it's a circle between the frog's legs. The water's dark an calm. Even a twitch from the frog'd've ruckled it. Ye can just see our two reflections each side of the moon.

A big seagull'll probably clamp the frog in its beak an flap off swallowin wi big gulps as it goes. That's their game the aul seagulls. No feelins at all. I seen it wi a stukkie once. This stukkie couldn't fly right. I put it on the grass for its maw to find. I'm flickin pebbles in the Burn an I sees this big gull flappin wi the stukkie in its mouth. It was horrible. I could hear the skweek skweek of the stukkie an the gull's beak crunchin through the feathers as it swept in big leaps up the sky. It landed on Kirk Chemicals an the gull an all its other gull pals tore the screamin stukkie to bits. I was sick in the Burn.

Gal's skwirtin the lighter petrol Mackenzie forgot an lightin it. This long rope of fire's goin out in front.

Flame-thrower whoosh, he's goin.

He fires it right over the bushes in a big curve. It's great wi the dark sky behind it. Like an evil rainbow. Ye can even see it reflectin in the Burn. I've nearly forgot Mackenzie already.

Gal writes mine an his names on the ground in petrol an lights it. # GAL DERRICK

burns like a tribal fire. Gal starts doin this Abbo dance round about me.

na na na ya na na na ya na na na ha ha ya na na na ya na na na ya na na

All the time he's squirtin petrol on the ground an lightin it. I'm trapped in a circle of fire. It's like the Johnny Cash record ma Da's always playin. Even if Gal is ma pal I starts gettin scared. His face's flickerin red an orange. Behind him the trees're black an the spaces between them's blacker. The end of the sun's all over the white peaks of the Slaggy like blood. An Gal's still goin,

If that's not bad enough Mackenzie comes back in ma head. Gal's terryfyin me.

Stop it Gal, I goes. But he keeps on goin.

Stop it! I shouts. *I'm feart!*

An he stops like nothin happened.

What ye gettin all het up about? You still scared of that Meccano Joe Guy? He says like he's the best pal ye could get.

Eh? I goes. His face has changed back to normal.

The mad fella? You still feart?

I just looks at him. I'm not sure – not sure at all.

Gal's eyes click into madness again an he starts the dance round me

chantin an squirtin a circle of petrol.

He lights it an leaves me bewildered in the middle. I'm not shoutin. For a wee minute I thinks he's goin to kill me. GAL!!?? That's it. Ma best pal's goin to kill me. I talks cos I'm scared shoutin'll make him mentaller. His eyes're flashin like a crazy crow.

Gal you're freakin me out.

He keeps dancin in trance madness.

Gal stop it. What about the Cyclepath? Meccano Joe. The Telly says he's near here.

He snaps back like nothin's happened again. He's laughin when he says it, *Christ! Mackenzie probably done him in.*

I lets out this laugh. Not a real laugh. A worried laugh. Now I don't know what's the most scary Gal, Mackenzie, or Meccano Joe. Weird. Gal starts usin his coax me down off somethin high voice.

Look we'll be OK. If we can survive Mackenzie we can survive anythin.

I'm still not sure. I don't trust him. I think he's been sniffin that glue. I give Gal a I'm still not sure look. He says nothin. I'm goin home. That's it!

I'm goin home Gal.

He gives me a look.

I'm goin home!

Ye can tell he's thinkin how to get me to stay. He's bitin his lip an his head's doin overtime. Ye'd think he'd try to tell me about some Great Spotted Pecker Bird's nest or somethin. But know what he does? He pulls out a wee tin of Evil Stick. See! I knew he was sniffin glue. I knew it.

Mackenzie's – fancy a sniff?

Me Sniffin Glue? *I'm goin home.* I goes.

Gal grabs ma soldiers.

C'mon just see what it's like?

No way Gal. You do it.

He tries the eggs in the nest trick.

Look! Mibbi... mibbi Mackenzie's burnt the Moorhen's?

An even if I sayed to ma da I'd get him one I was too feart. Thing's never felt right.

Too dodgy Gal. We'll just go home. Come back the morra. Eh? When it's light Gal. Eh?

I'm not really wantin to be wi Gal now cos of the funny dancin an the Abbo language. An sniffin the glue an not lettin on. I starts walkin away. He says nothin for a minute an then.

Alf Tupper – Tough of the Track!

He says it like he's askin for the last chip. I keep walkin – head down. What can I do wi him mad wi glue. He gives it another go.

Alf Tupper – Tough of the Track!

There's wind comin an ma feetsteps swishin on the soft grass. The wind bends round the trees in a quiet whisper.

Go home son Go homessssssssson, it's sayin. It sounds like ma da. Gal shouts. This time like he's accusin me of somethin.

Alf Tupper for fuck sake!!!!

I trip a bit but I keep walkin.

You're a shitebag Riley. D'ye know that. A shitebag!

His voice is pushin me away. A big black hand on ma back. I starts runnin.

A shitebag. That's you an me finished so it is. Finished!!!

I flicks round as I'm runnin. Gal gives me the fingers an slides in the trees that lead up to the Peak.

I'm batterin through the trees. Ma ears're great sometimes at tellin me somethin's up. I starts walkin an breathin wee. There's a light in the trees an I sneak up. I forwards bellyflap. It's Mackenzie. He's pourin this other pot of Evil Stick in a crisp poke. I'm back at the bit where he burnt me. I touch ma singed hair automatic an Mackenzie seems to smell me.

Sniff sniff, he's goin. Like a weasel. He peers right at me but he can't see nothin. The fire's makin a dark circle all about him. It's like the fire sucks all the light out the trees an throws it up in the air as flames. I'm absolute black an Mackenzie's red. He keeps poppin pills in his mouth an flingin them back wi Buckie.

Next thing his eyes light up like a good idea an he dashes for somethin the other side of the fire. Ma heart's in ma mouth. I think it's Gal but it's Gal's sling. He birls it round. He rubs his arse.

Bastard, he goes.

He's lookin about an listenin like anythin. He bends down again an picks up a load of flyin saucers. The ones I dumped.

Bastards! he says again. A bigger bastards than the last one. I shrink in the trees. I think he can see me. He's goin to spring through the flames any minute an rip me to bits.

He rubs his arse an curses us upside down.

SHIT! He takes a pure flaky on the trees. Then he's bootin the fire everywhere. Fire balls like meteorites're scorchin through the forest tracin a line of light an leavin paths of absolute darkness. Darkness like outer space. An a horrible quiet.

One of them lands away to ma left. In its scorch I see Gal paddin careful forward.

I starts creepin away. Mackenzie's still tellin the trees what he's goin to do to me an Gal when he gets us. He's choppin the branches wi his knife.

Slow down! I'm sayin but ma heart an ma breathin an ma feet're gettin faster an faster. I falls. Feet're near me so I stay. The ground smells like fear. Ma magination runs riot.

I magine a hand grabbin Gal's neck. It's Meccano Joe. An he's bashin this Meccano plane off Gal's head. Gal's head's dentin. But it's not dentin like a head. It's dentin like it's made out aluminium. Every whack wi the Meccano plane Gal's head crumples. Eventually his head's bashed right down his neck. His tongue's loppin out the top of his jumper an Meccano Joe's got it wi pliers. Gal escapes by rippin his own tongue out. Meccano's standin there wi the pliers an this hangin tongue dribblin wi slabbers an blood. Gal's bumpin into trees an blood squirtin out the top of his neck. It's horrible. Terryble.

I jumps up.

Gaaaaaaaaaaaaaaaaaaaaaaaaaaaaaaaaaal!!! I shouts.

The ground shudders wi Gal's feetprints comin to a stop. The planet jerks to a stop. All the trees bend forward a wee bit an then spring up straight again. I'm listenin for Gal an Mackenzie zooms right by me. Lookin. His eyes're red wi glue an mad. Pills an Buckie too. He's trippin over roots. Branches're slashin his face. Right next to me he passes. I can smell his stinkin breath. An glue. An petrol.

These other feet're runnin the other way. Must be Gal. I starts movin.

I'm runnin in the opposite way from Mackenzie.

Gaaaaaaaaaaaaaaaaaal!!!

This quiet happens. Nobody's runnin. Ye just know there's two people listenin. It's the quiet that's listenin – that's what it feels like. The quiet's a person. Next thing the best sound ever.

Derrrrrrrrriiiiiiiick!!!

It's Gal.

Ov-er hee-here.

Where are ye?

Keep shou-tin.

Alf Tupper Tough of the Track-ack-ack-ack-ack.

Billy Whizz right at his back-ack-ack-ack-ack.

Gal doesn't know Mackenzie's on our tail. Or the sling an the flyin saucers. We're dead. I can see Mackenzie in ma head smilin an comin back at our shoutin. It's a triangle. Me an Gal's at the bottom points an Mackenzie's at the big point. But he's comin an the triangle's shrinkin.

He's not daft Gal. He's headin away all the time an shoutin. Leadin me towards him. I pass through a clearin an **there it is!** – his body scratchin up the Peak. He's shinin in the moon. I bolt faster still shoutin an he's still answerin. Behind me deep in the trees Mackenzie's somewhere like a animal.

Gal's on the Peak when I get there. He's lookin out over the slag hills to the jewel carriageway. I can see the lines an curves of rubies an emeralds an white diamonds disappear into the distance. He's just about to start talkin to me about them an I buts in.

Gal Mackenzie's...

I'm tellin him when who's there laughin but Mackenzie. The Peak's like an upside down iron wi the pointed bit slopin up the sky. Gal's on the tip. It's miles to the ground an Mackenzie's got his knife out. It's a triangle again. Gal's at the top an me an Mackenzie's the other two points.

His boots're crunchin like lions' roars in the slag.

Where's yer sling now Gallacher? He goes jerkin to the left an stickin his hand out cos I moved. He's herdin us to the point.

Gal moves back one step sactly. But one step exactly's the edge. Some stones

fall

an hit the bottom.

Like in the films. Only this is real. Gal's froze. Trapped. Mackenzie staggers right up an puts the blade on his balls. Funny the things ye member. This Robin takes off an its wee red breast's like a flyin Sacred Heart. An I member its wings. When it takes off they make the sact same noise as a purrin cat. I'm just thinkin that when Mackenzie's voice creaks out.

Where's ma gear? Ma swedgers? Ma fags?

Gal can't move cos of the knife. Shadows're spreadin an unspreadin everywhere in the moonlight.

We've not got yer gear ya prick, I goes.

Well! Should've seen Mackenzie's face. He thinks about comin at me an members me an Gal's great at gettin away. But he's let the knife go a bit so Gal can talk.

What sling? What swedgers? Fags?

Embassy Tipped – Mint Cracknels – Whoppers – Aztecs – MB bars – Flyin fuckin Saucers... Where are they!!!???? It's the feartist I ever saw Gal.

He sticks the knife at Gal's neck. Blood's tricklin down. The trees're swishin about in the Slaggy below like dark green velvet.

The moon's a thin slice of cucumber stuck on a glass roof. It's lightin the Slaggy up like ripped white card against the blackboard in Art.

You done Columba ya bastard, I blurts out.

He turns an glares at me. He grins an shakes his head like he's proud of Columba. Then he remembers somethin. He gets Gal so he can shove his hand in his army jacket an he pulls out a handful of Moorhens' eggs.

I should've shot you in the head down the Gravy. C'mere, he goes.

I'm starin right at the eggs. There's burn marks on them. I starts walkin towards him. But he doesn't know about ma da an the Moorhens. He's surprised. He lets Gal flump. *C'mon,* he goes. I thinks Gal's goin to fall over but he rolls down the hill till Mackenzie stomps his boot on him. There's blood on Gal's neck an Mackenzie's knife is glintin. That's when he smiles again an starts crushin the eggs. There's yella an clear drippin in long slabbers through his fingers. Some of it's landin on Gal's face. Gal's breathin reminds me of ma da.

YEARHRHRHRG HGHG!

I lets out this amazin scream an runs at him like an upside-down L. Mackenzie's stunned. Even Gal looks up. I sticks the head right in his guts. Mackenzie oofs an goes backwards. I keeps shovin. Uphill. He's tryin to swing the knife down. But he's not got time. I keeps shovin. I shouts,

I was gettin a Moorhen's for ma da ya fucker...

His heel catches this stone. His arms go up an he drops the blade. His hands're searchin for things to grab. Nothin's ever grew on the Peak. He screams. He falls over the edge. Me an Gal do wide eyes at each other.

Mackenzie's face is all surprised when he puts his boot out into nothin. Smilin. Then screamin. His hands goin behind him tryin to find somethin. His head swingin down in a sick curve. The last thing I see is his boots.

THUD

He hits the bottom. There's this moanin an he's at the bottom shoutin for us to get an amblence. Gal phoned it an Mackenzie got took away up the Monklands. Mad thing is ma da got took into hospital sact same night as Mackenzie. Gal's maw telt us when we got home. I hightailed it up the Monklands.

When I got there ma da's breathin like a fish in a big oxygen tent an his eyes're pumpin out like he wants me to give him somethin. But I never had nothin. I'm standin there hopeless. I was goin to tell him all about the Moorhens an Mackenzie but ma maw says not to bother him wi the likes of that he's got enough on his plate as it is. He's not got long to go. All ma sisters're greetin an ma maw. She's shovin her arm under the plastic an holdin ma da's hand. There's a plastic surface nothin can get through. An a thin film of steam between them. An ma da starts greetin.

I don't know what happened. I just started singin. Everybody stopped an looked at me. Their mouths're wide open an black like universes wi no stars. The whole hospital stops.

Train whistle blowin
makes a sleepy noise
underneath the blankets
go all the girls and boys

I can sing nothin me. I can sing fuck all. People's amazed. The nurse's shoes've stopped squeakin outside in the corridor. I'm still singin. Nobody's even noticed ma hair.

♪Somewhere there is sunshine
somewhere there is rain
somewhere there is mornin town
many miles away

But then ma da smiles an then ma maw smiles. She calls me over. I can hardly see her for ma tears. She shoves ma arm under the tent. She starts fiddlin wi ma hair an smellin it. Ma da squeezes ma hand. An he looks at me an smiles again. That's when I knew everythin was alright about me not gettin the Moorhen's. Everythin was just fine.

Rockin rollin ridin, Da, I says, *right along the bay.*